Watts Isaac

The Poetical Works of Isaac Watts in Seven Volumes

With the Life of the Author. Vol. 1

Watts Isaac

The Poetical Works of Isaac Watts in Seven Volumes
With the Life of the Author. Vol. 1

ISBN/EAN: 9783337290962

Printed in Europe, USA, Canada, Australia, Japan

Cover: Foto ©Andreas Hilbeck / pixelio.de

More available books at **www.hansebooks.com**

DʳWATTS.

Engraved by Potter from an original Picture in the possession of Mʳ Abney Vaughan.

London Printed for John Bell British Library Strand May 17ᵗʰ 1782.

BELL'S EDITION
The POETS of GREAT BRITAIN
COMPLETE FROM
CHAUCER to CHURCHILL.

WATTS'S PSALMS
In vain the Rebel seeks to stand
In Judgment with the Pious race,
Psalm 1st

THE

POETICAL WORKS

OF

ISAAC WATTS, D.D.

IN SEVEN VOLUMES.

WITH THE LIFE OF THE AUTHOR.

Say, human Seraph! whence that charming force,
That flame, that foul, which animates each line,
And how it runs with fuch a graceful eafe,
Loaded with pond'rous fenfe?——We are here told,
When life its narrow round of years hath roll'd,
What 't is employsthe blefs'd, what makes their blifs;
Songs fuch as WATTS's are, and love like his.   GROVE.

Sov'reign of Sacred Verfe! accept the lays
Of a young bard that dares attempt thy praife.——
No vulgar themes thy pious Mufe engage,
No fcenes of luft pollute thy facred page :
You in majeftick numbers mount the fkies,
And meetdefcending angels as you rife,
Whofe juft applaufes charm the crowded groves,
And Addifon thy tuneful fong approves.
Soft harmony and manly vigour join
To form the beauties of each fprightly line,
For ev'ry grace of ev'ry Mufe is thine.   } BRITANNICUS.

VOL. I.

EDINBURG:
AT THE Apollo Press, BY THE MARTINS.
Anno 1782.

THE
POETICAL WORKS
OF
ISAAC WATTS, D.D.
VOL. I.

CONTAINING HIS

PSALMS OF DAVID,

Imitated in the Language of

THE NEW TESTAMENT,

And applied to

THE CHRISTIAN STATE AND WORSHIP,

WITH PREFACE, NOTES, INDEXES,

&c. &c. &c.

Luke xxiv. 44. All things must be fulfilled which were written in the Psalms concerning me
Heb. xi. 32. —— David, Samuel, and the Prophets, ver. 40. —— That they without us should not be made perfect.

Hail, heaven-born Muse! that with celestial flame
And high seraphick numbers durst attempt
To gain thy native skies —— With thought sublime
And high sonorous words thou sweetly sing'st
To thy immortal lyre. Amaz'd we view
The tow'ring height stupendous, while thou soar'd
Above the reach of vulgar eyes or thought,
Hymning th' Eternal Father.   STANDEN.

Seraphick heights I seem to gain
And sacred transports feel
While WATTS! to thy celestial strain
Surpris'd I listen still.

The gliding streams their course forbear
When I thy lays repeat,
The bending forest lends an ear,
The birds their notes forget.   PHILOMELA.

EDINBURG:
AT THE Apollo Press, BY THE MARTINS,
Anno 1782.

DR. ISAAC WATTS †.

I r has been fo ufual to prefix fome account of an author's life to his works, that many perfons would no
doubt be difappointed of their expectation, and would
look upon the book as imperfect, without fomething
of that fort. It is not becaufe there is no furviving
friend of the Doctor's who would willingly pay that
refpect to his memory as to write the hiftory of his
life that the reader is not gratified in this refpect with
fo large a narrative as he would probably defire, but
it is becaufe the Doctor himfelf while living difap-
proved it; for when he has been defired to leave fome
memoirs that might furnifh out fuch a hiftory he ab-
folutely declined it, and defired that his character
might ftand in the world merely as it would appear
in his Works. Befides, as the Doctor's feeble ftate of
health through the greater part of his life obliged him
to pafs the moft of his time in retirement from the
world, not fo many incidents and changes occurred
in his life (which was for the moft part led on in one
even track) as generally furnifh out a good part of
fuch hiftories; (and that by the way makes it truly
wonderful how he acquired fuch a knowledge of the

---

† Taken from the Account of Dr. Watts's Life and Character
prefixed to the quarto edition of his Works in fix vols. printed
in 1753.

world and of mankind as appears in his writings, and
it shews him to have been a very curious and judicious
observer of every thing that lay within his notice)
though yet an entertaining and useful narrative might
have been formed by intersperfing it with letters
which he wrote to his friends on various occasions,
many of which might probably have been picked up ;
but it is in deference to his judgment, and indeed in
compliance with his defire, that none of them are publifhed : for on the publication of fome letters to particular friends along with an author's life fome years
ago, the Doctor expreffed his difapprobation of fuch
a practice, and was pleafed to fay " that if he knew
" any body who would publifh his letters after he was
" dead he fhould not thank him for it." Thofe letters
muft therefore remain in the private hands of his
friends to whom they were infcribed, and by whom
many of them are prized more than gold. However,
in fome fort to comply with cuftom, as well as to pre-
ferve the memory of fo amiable a character and fo inftructive an example as Dr. Watts's was, it is thought
proper on this occafion to republifh the following brief
Memoirs of his Life and Character from his funeral
fermon preached by Dr. Jennings to the church of
which he was paftor Dec. 11. 1748.

" Dr. Ifaac Watts was born at Southampton July
17. 1674, of parents who were eminent for religion,
and were confiderable fufferers for confcience fake in

2

the perfecution of the Proteftant Diffenters in King
Charles IId's reign. The uncommon genius of this
their fon appeared betimes, for he began to learn Latin
at four years old, in the knowledge of which as well
as of the Greek language he made a fwift progrefs
under the care of the Rev. Mr. Pinhorne, a clergy-
man of the eftablifhed church, to whom the Doctor
has infcribed an ingenious Latin ode in his *Horæ Lyricæ*. He was early taken notice of for the fprightli-
nefs and vivacity of his wit, talents which too often
prove fatal fnares to young perfons; but he through
the diftinguifhing grace of God was not only pre-
ferved from criminal follies, but had a deep fenfe of
religion upon his heart betimes. In the year 1690 he
was fent up to London for academical education,
where he was placed under the tuition of the Rev.
Mr. Thomas Rowe, to whom alfo he has infcribed an
ode in his *Horæ Lyricæ*. I have been credibly informed
that while he refided in this college of learning his behaviour was not only fo inoffenfive that his tutor declared he never once gave him any occafion for reproof, but fo exemplary that he often propofed him
as a pattern to his other pupils for their imitation. In
the year 1693 he joined in communion with the church
of which his worthy tutor was paftor. When he had
finifhed his courfe of ftudies at the academy he return-
ed to his father's houfe, where he fpent two years
more in reading, meditation, and prayer, in order to

his being further qualified and fitted for that great work to which he was determined to devote his life, and of the awful importance of which he had a deep fenfe upon his mind. From hence he was invited in the year 1696, by that eminently pious and learned gentleman Sir John Hartopp Bart. deceafed, to refide in his family at Stoke-Newington, as tutor to his fon, the prefent Sir John, where he continued four years, and where his behaviour won him fuch efteem and refpect as laid the foundation of that intimate friend-fhip which fubfifted between his worthy pupil and him to the day of his death.

But while he affifted Sir John's ftudies he did not neglect his own; for not only did he further improve himfelf in thofe branches of learning in which more e-fpecially he affifted his pupil, but applied himfelf to the reading of the Scriptures in the original tongues, and the beft commentators both critical and practical.

He began to preach on his birthday 1698, and was the fame year chofen Affiftant to the Rev. Dr. Ifaac Chauncy, then paftor of this church: but his publick labours, which met with general acceptance, were foon after interrupted by a threatening illnefs for five months, which was thought to be occafioned by the fervour of his zeal in preaching the glorious gofpel of Chrift. However that did not difcourage him from returning to his delightful work as foon as God was pleafed to reftore his health.

In January 1701 he received a call from this church to succeed Dr. Chauncy in the pastoral office, which he signified his acceptance of the very day that King William died, notwithstanding the discouraging prospect which that event gave to men of his profession, and the fears with which it filled the hearts of Protestant Dissenters at that time. But he had " set his " hand to the plough, and would not look back :" accordingly he was solemnly ordained to the pastoral office 18th March following.

But the joy of the church in their happy settlement was soon after damped by his being seized with a painful and threatening illness, which laid him by for some time, and from which he recovered by slow degrees; upon which they saw it needful to provide him with a stated Assistant; accordingly the Rev. Mr. Samuel Price, your present worthy pastor, was chosen to that service in July 1703.

But notwithstanding his publick labours were by this means eased his health remained very fluctuating and tender for some years. However as it increased he renewed his diligence in fulfilling his ministry; and how were you delighted and edified with his sermons in publick, and with his entertaining and profitable conversation in the visits which he made to your families! It was in this season of his more confirmed health that he formed a society of the younger members of his church for prayer and religious conference, to whom he delivered the substance of that excellent

book which he afterwards publifhed under the title of
A Guide to Prayer. Now he went on without any
confiderable interruption in his work, and with great
fuccefs and profperity to his church, till the year 1712,
when in the month of September he was vifited with
a violent fever which broke his conftitution, and left
fuch weaknefs upon his nerves as continued with him
in fome meafure to his dying day. Upon this occafion
" prayer was made without ceafing of the church un-
" to God for him :" feveral days of prayer were kept
on his account, in which many of his brethren in the
miniftry affifted, and wreftled earneftly with God for
the continuance of fo valuable a life; and God has been
gracioufly pleafed to anfwer their prayers by adding
to his life more than thirty-fix years, the moft of them
years though of feeble health yet of eminent ufefulnefs to his church and to the world. It was not till
October 1716 that he was able to return to his publick miniftry. In the mean-time his Affiftant Mr.
Price was, at his defire, and upon his recommendation,
chofen by the church to be joint paftor with him, to
which office he was ordained March 3, 1713. I hope
I may be allowed, without offence or appearance of
flattery, to recite a claufe in Dr. Watts's laft will in
teftimony of that inviolable friendfhip which has always fubfifted between your two worthy paftors, and
which has contributed fo much to their mutual comfort and honour, and to your eftablifhment and edifi-
cation. Dr. Watts ftyles him " His faithful friend and

" companion in the labours of the miniftry;" and men-
tions a legacy that he leaves him " as only a fmall tefti-
" mony of his great affection for him, on account of
" his fervices of love during the many harmonious
" years of their fellowfhip in the work of the gofpel."

But though this long interval of ficknefs was on
fome accounts a very melancholy feafon, yet a kind
Providence made it to be the happieft era of his life,
as it was the occafion of introducing him into the family of a late excellent perfon†, who on a principle
of the moft generous friendfhip and compaffion took
him, in a very languifhing ftate of health, to his own
houfe, where from that moment to the day of his
death he was abundantly fupplied with all that could
minifter either to the convenience or fatisfaction of
his life; for though this remarkable friend of minifters
of the church of God and of his country died in the
year 1722, the benevolent fpirit he manifefted fur-
vived in his worthy relict, and was inherited by his
children. It would be prefumption in me to attempt
to recount the numberlefs inftances of that " gene-
" rous and tender care (as the Doctor expreffes it in
" his laft will) fhown him by her ladyfhip and her fa-
" mily in his long illnefs many years ago, when he
" was capable of no fervice, and alfo of her eminent
" friendfhip and goodnefs during his continuance in
" the family ever fince;" yet this I will venture to
fay, in allufion to the bleffing which our Lord pro-

† Sir Thomas Abney Knight, and Alderman of London.

nounced on the good woman in the gospel who had bestowed a box of precious ointment on him, that wheresoever Dr. Watts's Works are read or his name remembered that of Abney ought not to be forgotten.

In the year 1728 the universities of Edinburgh and Aberdeen in Scotland did in a most respectful manner, without his knowledge, confer the degree of Doctor in Divinity on him, and on some others of his brethren.

His last sickness was rather a decay of nature, worn out with age and labours, than any particular distemper, therefore it was lingering and long; the springs of life were unbending by degrees, till at length the earthly tabernacle fell quite to decay, and was put off by the immortal spirit. And thus after a life of eminent service both of God and his generation he fell asleep in Jesus Nov. 25. 1748, in the seventy-fifth year of his age.

It would require a masterly hand to draw the portrait of this great man in its full proportion and proper colours, a task I was never equal to, and am least of all now, when I doubt not but your hearts will in some measure tell you what mine feels upon the mention of his name, and upon calling the remembrance of him to mind: however I will endeavour to present you with an imperfect sketch of some of the principal features.

The natural strength of his genius, which he cultivated and improved by a very considerable acquaintance with the most celebrated writers both ancient and modern, had enriched his mind with a large and uncommon store of just sentiments and useful knowledge of various kinds, for his soul was too noble and large to be confined within narrow limits; he could not be content to leave any path of learning untried, nor to rest in a total ignorance of any science the knowledge of which might be for his own improvement, or might any ways tend to enlarge his capacity of being useful to others.

Though that which gave him the most remarkable preeminence was the extent and sublimity of his imagination, yet how few have excelled or even equalled him in quickness of apprehension and solidity of judgment? and having also a faithful memory to retain what he collected from the labours of others, he was able to pay it back again into the common treasury of learning with a large increase. I question whether any author before him did ever appear with reputation on such a variety of subjects as he has done, both as a prose writer and a poet. However this I may venture to say, that there is no man now living of whose works so many have been dispersed both at home and abroad, that are in such constant use, and translated into such a variety of languages, many of which will I doubt not remain more durable monuments of his great talents than any representation I can make of them though it were to be graven on pillars of brass. Thus did he shine as an ingenious man and a scholar.

But we are further to obferve him in a more exalted point of view for our inftruction and imitation; I
mean as a Chriftian, in which character he fhone
brighteft of all; and it is hard to fay what grace or
virtue was moft confpicuous in him and moft charac-
teriftick of him.

Pure and undiffembled piety was the fettled habit
and conftant drefs of his mind; and though he loved
and enjoyed much retirement, yet did he not thereby
contract any thing of an affected ftiffnefs or monkifh
aufterity, but on the contrary, the fatisfaction and
pleafure that he found in communion with God in
folitude made him the more eafy and cheerful in his
converfe with men, and feemed to enlighten his very
countenance.

His humility was like a deep fhade, if I may fo exprefs it, that fet off his other graces and virtues and
made them fhine with a brighter luftre; and as this
grace had a mighty influence on his heart and temper, fo it had no little effect in forming his fentiments;
for he never thought he could be laid too low, as a
creature or a finner, that he might do honour to the
perfections and grace of God; and from hence in a
great meafure arofe that high efteem which he had
for the Chriftian difpenfation, which is fo apparently
calculated to exalt God and to humble man. Nor was
his humility lefs confpicuous in his outward carriage
and behaviour towards others; from hence flowed
that condefcenfion and gentlenefs, that humanity and

kindnefs, that could not but endear him to all who had
the pleafure of converfing with him, and which rendered him truly venerable in a much higher degree than all
the honours and applaufes he received from the world.
In fhort, his defcription of this grace, which he has fo
beautifully exemplified in the character of St. Paul †,
feems to be but a tranfcript of his own heart and life.

In clofe connexion with the grace of humility were
to be feen his candour and charity, for which he was
remarkably eminent. The love that glowed in his
heart to his Saviour conftrained him cordially to em-
brace all whom he efteemed to be his genuine dif-
ciples; and no party names nor variety of fentiments
in matters of doubtful difputation, nor of practice in
modes of worfhip, could divide him in affection from
fuch as he had reafon to hope loved our Lord Jefus
Chrift in fincerity; accordingly he maintained a free
and friendly correfpondence with Chriftians of different parties and denominations. Though he judged
the principles of the moderate Nonconformifts moft
favourable to Chriftian liberty and the rights of confcience, and their forms of worfhip moft agreeable to
the fimplicity of the gofpel, yet he had a high vene-
ration for the perfons and writings of many in the
eftablifhed church, as many of them both in higher
and lower ftations had for him and his writings. And

---

† Humility reprefented in the Character of St. Paul. By
Ifaac Watts, D. D.

I speak it to the distinguished honour and praise of some very reverend personages of that communion, as well as to his, that they frequently presented him with their works and accepted of his in return; on which, as well as on other occasions, very serious and affectionate letters have passed between them for the strengthening each others hands in the cause of our common Christianity.

What his sentiments were as to the peculiar doctrines of the gospel you who have statedly attended on his ministry well know, and none need be ignorant who will peruse his writings.

Though he occasionally engaged in the controversies of the day, it was evidently with a view to heal and reconcile disputes amongst Christians rather than to make proselytes to any party; and however any may in some matters differ from him in judgment, all must allow that he wrote on such occasions with such a spirit of meekness and love as is truly instructive and exemplary.

Nor did love and goodness only dwell in his heart, but flowed out from thence in liberal and beneficent actions; for I am credibly informed that from the time he was received into Sir Thomas Abney's family he constantly devoted a fifth part of his income to charitable uses.

It is no wonder that a man thus richly furnished with gifts and graces was an admired preacher. Though his stature was low and his bodily presence but weak, yet his preaching was weighty and powerful. There was a certain dignity and fpirit in his very afpect when he appeared in the pulpit that commanded attention and awe; and when he fpoke, fuch ftrains of truly Chriftian eloquence flowed from his lips, and thefe fo apparently animated with zeal for God and the moft tender concern for your fouls and their everlafting falvation, as one would think could not be cafily flighted or refifted.

Though his publick labours for your good were frequently interrupted by ficknefs, yet was he not even in thofe intervals laid wholly afide from his ufefulnefs, for not only was his exemplary patience and refignation to the will of God in thofe feafons of his fuffering very inftructive, but fome of the fineft and moft ufeful productions of his pen, as particularly a good part of his Imitation of the Pfalms of David, owe their birth to thofe feafons of conftrained retirement.

In his laft ficknefs the active and fprightly powers of his nature failed him, that is, they were gradually doing fo for two or three years before his deceafe ; yet his truft in God through Jefus the Mediator remained unfhaken to the laft. He has been heard to fay, " I " blefs God I can lie down with comfort at night, not " being folicitous whether I awake in this world or " another." And again, " I fhould be glad to read " more, yet not in order to be more confirmed in the " truth of the Chriftian religion or in the truth of its

B iij

" promifes, for I believe them enough to venture an
" eternity on them." When he was almoft worn out
and broken down by his infirmities he obferved, in
converfation with a friend, that " he remembered an
" aged minifter ufed to fay that the moft learned and
" knowing Chriftians when they come to die have
" only the fame plain promifes of the gofpel for their
" fupport as the common and unlearned; and fo, faid
" he, I find it: it is the plain promifes of the gofpel
" that are my fupport, and I blefs God they are plain
" promifes, that do not require much labour and pains
" to underftand them, for I can do nothing now but
" look into my Bible for fome promife to fupport me,
" and live upon that." When he has found his fpirit
tending to impatience, and ready to complain that he
could only lead a mere animal life, he would check
himfelf thus, " The bufinefs of a Chriftian is to bear
" the will of God as well as to do it. If I were in health
" I could only be doing that, and that I may do now.
" The beft thing in obedience is a regard to the will
" of God, and the way to that is to get our inclina-
" tions and averfions as much mortified as we can."
With fuch a calm and peaceful mind, with fuch a
blefied and lively hope, did this faithful fervant of
Chrift wait for his Mafter's fummons till the long-
wifhed for period came, and then he went to reft from
his labours where his works follow him."

THE PREFACE,

An Inquiry into the right way of fitting The Book of Psalms for Christian Worship.

THOUGH the Pfalms of David are a work of admirable and divine compofure, though they contain the nobleft fentiments of piety, and breathe a moft exalted fpirit of devotion, yet when the beft of Chriftians attempt to fing many of them in our common tranflation that fpirit of devotion vanifhes and is loft, the pfalm dies upon their lips, and they feel fcarce any thing of the holy pleafure.

If I were to render the reafons of it I would give this for one of the chief, namely, that the royal Pfalmift here expreffes his own concerns in words exactly fuited to his own thoughts, agreeable to his own perfonal character, and in the language of his own religion : this keeps all the fprings of pious paffion awake, when ev'ry line and fyllable fo nearly affects himfelf; this naturally raifes in a devout mind a more lively and tranfporting worfhip; but when we who are Chriftians fing the fame lines we exprefs nothing but the character, the concerns, and the religion, of the Jewifh king; while our own circumftances and our own religion (which are fo widely different from his) have little to do in the facred fong, and our affections want fomething of property or intereft in the words to awaken them at firft and to keep them lively.

If this attempt of mine, through the divine blefling, become fo happy as to remove this great inconvenience, and to introduce warm devotion into this part of divine worfhip, I fhall efteem it an honourable fervice done to the church of Chrift.

It is neceffary therefore that I fhould here inform my readers at large, what the titlepage expreffes in a fhorter way, and affure them that they are not to expect in this book an exact tranflation of The Pfalms of David ; for if I had not conceived a different defign from all that have gone before me in this work I had never attempted a fervice fo full of labour, though I muft confefs it has not wanted its pleafure too.

In order to give a plain account of my prefent undertaking I fhall firft reprefent the methods that my predeceffors have followed in their verfions; in the next place I hope to make it evident that thofe methods can never attain the nobleft and higheft ends of Chriftian pfalmody; and then defcribe the courfe that I have taken, different from them all, together with fome brief hints of the reafons that induced me to it.

Firft, I will reprefent the methods that my predeceffors have followed. I have feen above twenty verfions of the Pfalter by perfons of richer and meaner ta-

lents, and how various foever their profeffions and
their prefaces are, yet in the performances they all feem
to aim at this one point, namely, to make the Hebrew
Pfalmift only fpeak Englifh and keep all his own characters ftill. Wherefoever the pfalm introduces him
as a foldier or a prophet, as a fhepherd or a great mufician, as a king on the throne, or as a fugitive in the
wildernefs, the tranflators ever reprefent him in the
fame circumftances. Some of them lead an affembly
of common Chriftians to worfhip God as near as poffible in thofe very words; and they generally agree
alfo to perform and repeat that worfhip in the ancient
Jewifh forms wherever the Pfalmift ufes them.

There are feveral pfalms indeed which have fcarce
any thing in them perfonal or peculiar to David or
the Jews, fuch as Pfalm i. xix. xxv. xxvii. lxvii. c. i. &c.
and thefe, if tranflated into the plain national language, are very proper materials for pfalmody in all
times and places; but there are but a few of this kind
in comparifon of the great number which have fomething of perfonal concerns, prophetical darkneffes,
Hebraifms, or Jewifh affairs, mingled with them.

I confefs Mr. Milburn and Mr. Darby (though
in very different verfe) have now and then given an
evangelick turn to the Hebrew fenfe; and Dr. Patrick hath gone fo much beyond them in this refpect
that he hath made ufe of the prefent language of Chriftians in feveral pfalms, and left out many of the Ju-

daifms. This is the thing that hath introduced him
into the favour of fo many religious affemblies; even
thofe very perfons that have an averfion to fing any
thing in worfhip but David's Pfalms have been led
infenfibly to fall in with Dr. Patrick's performance
by a relifh of pious pleafure, never confidering that
his work is by no means a juft tranflation, but a paraphrafe; and there are fcarce any that have departed
farther from the infpired words of Scripture than he
hath often done, in order to fuit his thoughts to the
ftate and worfhip of Chriftianity. This I efteem his
peculiar excellency in thofe pfalms wherein he has
practifed it; this I have made my chief care and bufinefs in every pfalm, and have attempted at leaft to
exceed him in this as well as in the art of verfe, and
yet I have often kept nearer to the text.

But after all this good man hath fuffered himfelf fo
far to be carried away by cuftom as to make all the
other perfonal characters and circumftances of David
appear ftrong and plain except that of a Jew, and many of them he has reprefented in ftronger and plainer
terms than the original. This will appear to any one
that compares thefe following texts in Dr. Patrick
with the Bible, namely, Pfalm iv. 2. and ix. 4, 5. and
xviii. 43. and li. 4. and lx. 6, 7. and ci. 1. cxli. 6. and
cxliii. 3. and feveral others: fo that it is hard to find
even in his verfion fix or eight ftanzas together in any
pfalm (that has perfonal or national affairs in it) fo fit

to be affumed by a vulgar Chriftian, or fo proper to
be fung by a whole congregation. This renders the
due performance of pfalmody every where difficult to
him that appoints the verfes, but it is extremely trou-
blefome in thofe affemblies where the pfalm is fung
without reading it line by line, which yet is beyond
all exception the trueft and the beft method; for
in this way of finging there can be no omiffion of a
verfe, though it be never fo improper; but the whole
church muft run down to the next divifion of the pfalm,
and fing all that comes next to their lips, till the Clerk
puts them to filence : or to remedy this inconvenience, if a wife man leads the fong he dwells always
upon four or five-and-twenty pieces of fome felect
pfalms, though the whole hundred and fifty lie before
him; and he is forced to run that narrow round ftill
for want of larger provifion fuited to our prefent circumftances.

I might here alfo remark to what a hard fhift the
minifter is put to find proper hymns at the celebra-
tion of the Lord's Supper, where the people will fing
nothing but out of David's pfalmbook. How perpe-
tually do they repeat fome part of the xxiii. or cxviii.
pfalm? and confine all the glorious joy and melody
of that ordinance to a few obfcure lines, becaufe the
tranflators have not indulged an evangelical turn to
the words of David? no not in thofe very places
where the Jewifh Pfalmift feems to mean the gofpel;

but as excellent a poet as he was he was not able to
speak it plain, by reason of the infancy of that difpenfation, and longs for the aid of a Chriftian writer;
though, to fpeak my own fenfe freely, I do not think
David ever wrote a pfalm of fufficient glory and fweetnefs to reprefent the bleffings of this holy inftitution
of Chrift, even though it were explained by a copious
commentator; therefore it is my opinion that other
fpiritual fongs fhould fometimes be ufed to render
Chriftian pfalmody complete. But this is not my prefent bufinefs, and I have written on this fubject elfe-
where.

To proceed to the fecond part of my Preface, which
is to fhew how infufficient a ftrict tranflation of the
Pfalms is to attain the defigned end.

There are feveral fongs of this royal author that
feem improper for any perfon befides himfelf, fo that
I cannot believe that the whole book of Pfalms (even
in the original) was appointed by God for the ordinary and conftant worfhip of the Jewifh fanctuary of
the fynagogues, though feveral of them might be often fung, much lefs are they all proper for a Chriftian
church; yet the way of a clofe tranflation of this
whole book of Hebrew Pfalms for Englifh and Chriftian pfalmody has generally obtained among us.

Some pretend it is but a juft refpect for the Holy
Scriptures, for they have imbibed a fond opinion
from their very childhood that nothing is to be fung

at church but the inspired writings, how different so-
ever the sense is from our present state. But this opinion has been taken upon trust by the most part of
its advocates, and borrowed chiefly from education,
custom, and the authority of others, which if duly
examined will appear to have been built upon too
slight and feeble foundations: the weakness of it I
shall shew more at large in another place: but it appears of itself more eminently inconsistent in those
persons that scruple to address God in prose in any
precomposed forms whatsoever; and they give this
reason, because they cannot be fitted to all our present
occasions; and yet in verse they confine their addresses
to such forms as were fitted chiefly for Jewish worshippers, and for the special occasions of David the
king.

Others maintain that a strict and scrupulous confinement to the sense of the original is necessary to do
justice to the royal author; but in my judgment the
royal author is most honoured when he is made most
intelligible, and when his admirable composures are
copied in such language as gives light and joy to the
saints that live two thousand years after him; whereas such a mere translation of all his verse into English
to be sung in our worship seems to darken our religion; by running back again to Judaism it damps our
delight, and almost forbids the Christian worshipper
to pursue the song. How can we assume to ourselves

all his words in our perfonal or publick addreffes to God when our condition of life, our time, place, and religion, are fo vaftly different from thofe of David?

I grant it is neceffary and proper that in tranflating every part of Scripture for our reading or hearing the fenfe of the original fhould be exactly and faithfully reprefented, for there we learn what God fays to us in his word; but in finging for the moft part the cafe is altered; for as the greateft number of the Pfalms are devotional, and there the Pfalmifts exprefs their own perfonal or national concerns, fo we are taught by their example what is the chief defign of pfalmody, namely, that we fhould reprefent our own fenfe of things in finging, and addrefs ourfelves to God expreffing our own cafe; therefore the words fhould be fo far adapted to the general ftate of the worfhippers as that we might feldom fing thofe expreffions in which we have no concern; or at leaft our tranflators of the Pfalms fhould obferve this rule, that when the peculiar circumftances of ancient faints are formed into a fong for our prefent and publick ufe, they fhould be related rather in an hiftorical manner, and not retain the perfonal pronouns *I* and *We* where the tranfactions cannot belong to any of us, nor be applied to our perfons, churches, or nation.

Mofes, Deborah, and the princes of Ifrael David, Afaph, and Habakkuk, and all the faints under the Jewifh ftate; fung their own joys and victories, their

own hopes, and fears, and deliverances, as I hinted
before; and why muſt we under the goſpel ſing nothing elſe but the joys, hopes, and fears, of Aſaph and
David? why muſt Chriſtians be forbid all other melody but what ariſes from the victories and deliverances of the Jews? David would have thought it very
hard to have been confined to the words of Moſes,
and ſung nothing elſe on all his rejoicing days but
the drowning of Pharaoh in the xvth of Exodus. He
might have ſuppoſed it a little unreaſonable, when he
had peculiar occaſions of mournful muſick, if he had
been forced to keep cloſe to Moſes's prayer in the
xcth pſalm, and always ſung over the ſhortneſs of human life, eſpecially if he were not permitted the liberty of a paraphraſe: and yet the ſpecial concerns
of David and Moſes were much more akin to each
other than ours are to either of them; and they were
both of the ſame religion, but ours is very different.

It is true that David has left us a richer variety of
holy ſongs than all that went before him, but rich as it
is it is ſtill far ſhort of the glorious things that we Chriſtians have to ſing before the Lord. We and our churches have our own ſpecial affairs as well as they: now if
by a little turn of their words, or by the change of a
ſhort ſentence, we may expreſs our own meditations,
joys, and deſires, in the verſe of thoſe ancient Pſal-
miſts, why ſhould we be forbid this ſweet privilege?
why ſhould we, under the Chriſtian diſpenſation, be

C ij

tied up to forms more than the Jews themselves were, and such as are much more improper for our age and state too? Let us remember that the very power of singing was given to human nature chiefly for this purpose, that our own warmest affections of soul might break out into natural or divine melody, and that the tongue of the worshipper might express his own heart.

I confess it is not unlawful nor absurd for a person of knowledge and skill in divine things to sing any part of the Jewish psalmbook and consider it merely as the word of God, from which by wise meditation he may draw some pious inferences for his own use, for instruction is allowed to be one end of psalmody; but where the words are obscure Hebraisms, or where the poet personates a Jew, a soldier, or a king, speaking to himself or to God, this mode of instruction in a song seems not so natural or easy even to the most skilful Christian, and it is almost impracticable to the greatest part of mankind; and both the wise and the weak must confess this, that it does by no means raise their own devotion so well as if they were speaking in their own persons and expressing their own sense: besides that the weaker Christian is ready to chime in with the words he sings, and use them as his own, though they are never so foreign to his purpose.

Now though it cannot be that a large book of lively devotions should be so framed as to have every line perfectly suited to all the circumstances of every wor-

fhipper, but after the writer's utmoft care there will
ftill be room for Chriftian wifdom to exercife the
thoughts aright in finging, when the words feem improper to our particular cafe, yet as far as poffible
every difficulty of this kind fhould be removed, and
fuch fentences fhould by no means be chofen which
can fcarce be ufed in their proper fenfe by any that
are prefent.

I could never perfuade myfelf that the beft way to
raife a devout frame in plain Chriftians was to bring
a king or a captain into their churches, and let him
lead and dictate the worfhip in his own ftyle of royal-
ty, or in the language of a field of battle. Does every
menial fervant in the affembly know how to ufe thefe
words devoutly, namely, " When I receive the con-
" gregation I will judge uprightly, Pfalm lxxv. 2.
" A bow of fteel is broken by mine arms.——As foon
" as they hear of me they fhall obey me," Pfalm xviii.
34. 44.? Would I encourage a Parifh-clerk to ftand up
in the midft of a country church and bid all the people join with his words, and fay, " I will praife thee
" upon a pfaltery;" or, " I will open my dark faying
" upon the harp?" when even our cathedrals fing
only to the found of an organ, moft of the meaner
churches can have no mufick but the voice, and others
will have none befides. Why then muft all who will
fing a pfalm at church ufe fuch words as if they were
to play upon the harp and pfaltery, when thoufands

C iij

never faw fuch an inftrument, and know nothing of the art?.

You will tell me perhaps that when you take thefe expreffions upon your lips you mean only that you will worfhip God according to his appointment now, even as David worfhipped him in his day according to God's appointment then. But why will ye confine yourfelves to fpeak one thing and mean another? why muft we be bound up to fuch words as can never be addreffed to God in their own fenfe? and fince the heart of a Chriftian cannot join herein with his lips, why may not his lips be led to fpeak his heart? Experience itfelf has often fhewn that it interrupts the holy melody, and fpoils the devotion of many a fincere good man or woman, when in the midft of the fong fome fpeeches of David have been almoft impofed upon their tongues where he relates his own troubles, his banifhment, or peculiar deliverances, where he fpeaks like a Jewifh prince, a mufician, or a prophet, or where the fenfe is fo obfcure that it cannot be underftood without a learned commentator.

Here I may with courage addrefs myfelf to the heart and confcience of many pious and obferving Chriftians, and afk them whether they have not found a moft divine pleafure in finging when the words of the pfalm have happily expreffed their frame of foul? Have you not felt a new joy fpring within you when you could fpeak your own defires and hopes, your own

faith, love, and zeal, in the language of the holy
Pfalmift? have not your fpirits taken wing and mount-
ed up near to God and glory with the fong of David
on your tongue? but on a fudden the Clerk has propofed the next line to your lips with dark fayings and
prophecies, with burnt-offerings or hyffop, with new
moons, and trumpets, and timbrels in it, with confef-
fions of fins which you never committed, with complaints of forrows which you never felt, curfing fuch
enemies as you never had, giving thanks for fuch victories as you never obtained, or leading you to fpeak
in your own perfons of things, places, and actions,
that you never knew; and how have all your fouls
been difcompofed at once, and the ftrings of harmony
all untuned! You could not proceed in the fong with
your hearts, and your lips have funk their joy, and
faltered in the tune; you have been balked and afha-
med, and knew not whether it were beft to be filent or
to follow on with the Clerk and the multitude, and
fing with cold devotion, and perhaps in darknefs too,
without thought or meaning.

Left it be replied here that to prevent this inconvenience fuch pfalms or fentences may be always o-
mitted by him that leads the fong, or may have a more
ufeful turn given in the mind of thofe that fing; but
I anfwer, fince fuch pfalms or fentences are not to be
fung, they may be as well omitted by the tranflator,
or may have a more ufeful turn given in the verfe

than is poffible for all the fingers to give on a fudden in their minds : and this is all that I contend for.

I come therefore to the third thing I propofed, and that is, to explain my own defign, which in fhort is this, namely, to accommodate the Book of Pfalms to Chriftian worfhip; and in order to this it is neceffary to diveft David and Afaph, &c. of every other character but that of a Pfalmift and a faint, and to make them always fpeak the common fenfe of a Chriftian.

Attempting the work with this view, I have entirely omitted fome whole pfalms, and large pieces of many others, and have chofen out of all of them fuch parts only as might eafily and naturally be accommodated to the various occafions of the Chriftian life, or at leaft might afford us fome beautiful allufion to Chriftian affairs : thefe I have copied and explained in the general ftyle of the Gofpel; ner have I confined my expreffions to any particular party or opinion, that in words prepared for publick worfhip, and for the lips of multitudes, there might not be a fyllable offenfive to fincere Chriftians, whofe judgments may differ in the leffer matters of religion.

Where the Pfalmift ufes fharp invectives againft his perfonal enemies I have endeavoured to turn the edge of them againft our fpiritual adverfaries, fin, Satan, and temptation; where the flights of his faith and love are fublime I have often funk the expreffions within the reach of an ordinary Chriftian ; where the words imply some peculiar wants or distresses, joys or blessings, I have used words of greater latitude and comprehension, suited to the general circumstances of men.

. Where the original runs in the form of prophecy concerning Christ and his salvation I have given an historical turn to the sense. There is no necessity that we should always sing in the obscure and doubtful style of prediction when the things foretold are brought into open light by a full accomplishment. Where the writers of the New Testament have cited or alluded to any part of the Psalms I have often indulged the liberty of paraphrase, according to the words of Christ or his apostles; and surely this may be esteemed the word of God still, though borrowed from several parts of the holy Scripture; where the Psalmist describes religion by the fear of God I have often joined faith and love to it; where he speaks of the pardon of sin through the mercies of God I have added the blood or merits of a Saviour; where he talks of sacrificing goats or bullocks I rather chuse to mention the sacrifice of Christ, the Lamb of God: when he attends the ark with shouting into Zion I sing the ascension of my Saviour into heaven, or his presence in his church on earth; where he promises abundance of wealth, honour, and long life, I have changed some of these typical blessings for grace, glory, and life eternal, which are brought to light by the gospel, and promi-

fed in the New Teſtament; and I am fully ſatisſied
that more honour is done to our bleſſed Saviour by
ſpeaking his name, his graces and actions, in his own
language, according to the brighter diſcoveries he hath
now made, than by going back again to the Jewiſh
forms of worſhip and the language of types and figures.

All men will confeſs this is juſt and neceſſary in
preaching and praying, and I cannot find a reaſon why
we ſhould not ſing praiſes alſo in a manner agreeable
to the preſent and more glorious diſpenſation. No man
can be perſuaded that to read a ſermon of the royal
preacher out of the book of Eccleſiaſtes, or a prayer out
of Ezra or Daniel, is ſo edifying to a Chriſtian church
(though they were inſpired) as a well compoſed prayer
or ſermon delivered in the uſual language of the goſpel
of Chriſt : and why ſhould the very words of the Sweet
Singer of Iſrael be eſteemed ſo neceſſary to Chriſtian
pſalmody, and the Jewiſh ſtyle ſo much preferable to
the evangelical, in our religious ſongs of praiſe ?

Now ſince it appears ſo plain that the Hebrew Pſal-
ter is very improper to be the preciſe matter and ſtyle
of our ſongs in a Chriſtian church, and ſince there is
very good reaſon to believe that it is left us not only
as a moſt valuable part of the word of God for our faith
and practice, but as an admirable and divine pattern
of ſpiritual ſongs and hymns under the goſpel, I have
choſen rather to *imitate* than to *tranſlate* ; and thus to

compose a Psalmbook for Christians after the manner
of the Jewish Psalter.

If I could be persuaded that nothing ought to be sung
in worship but what was of immediate inspiration from
God, surely I would recommend anthems only, namely,
the Psalms themselves, as we read them in the Bible,
set to musick as they are sung by choristers in our ca-
thedral churches, for these are nearest to the words of
inspiration, and we must depart far from those words
if we turn them into rhyme and metre of any sort; and
upon the foot of this argument even the Scotch version,
which has been so much commended for its approach
to the original, would be unlawful as well as others.

But since I believe that any divine sentence or Christian verse, agreeable to Scripture, may be sung, though
it be composed by men uninspired, I have not been so
curious and exact in striving every where to express
the ancient sense and meaning of David, but have rather expressed myself as I may suppose David would
have done had he lived in the days of Christianity; and
by this means perhaps I have sometimes hit upon the
true intent of the spirit of God in those verses farther
and clearer than David himself could ever discover, as
St. Peter encourages me to hope, 1 Peter i. 11, 12.
where he acknowledges that the ancient prophets, who
foretold of the grace that should come to us, were in
some measure ignorant of this great salvation; for
though they testified of the sufferings of Christ and his

glory, yet they were forced to search and inquire after the meaning of what they spake or wrote. In several other places I hope my reader will find a natural exposition of many a dark and doubtful text, and some new beauties and connexions of thought discovered in the Jewish poet, though not in the language of a Jew. In all places I have kept my grand design in view, and that is, to teach my author to speak like a Christian; for why should I now address God my Saviour in a song with burnt-sacrifices of fatlings, and with the fat of rams? why should I pray to be sprinkled with hyssop, or recur to the blood of bullocks and goats? why should I bind my sacrifice with cords to the horns of an altar, or sing the praises of God to high sounding cymbals, when the gospel has shewn me a nobler atonement for sin, and appointed a purer and more spiritual worship? why must I join with David in his legal or prophetick language to curse my enemies, when my Saviour in his sermons has taught me to love and bless them? why may not a Christian omit all those passages of the Jewish Psalmist that tend to fill the mind with overwhelming sorrows, despairing thoughts, or bitter personal resentments, none of which are well suited to the spirit of Christianity, which is a dispensation of hope, and joy, and love? what need is there that I should wrap up the shining honours of my Redeemer in the dark and shadowy language of a religion that is now for ever abolished, especially when Christians are so vehemently warned in the Epistles of St. Paul against a judaizing spirit in their worship as well as doctrine? and what fault can there be in enlarging a little on the more useful subjects in the style of the gospel, where the psalm gives any occasion, since the whole religion of the Jews is censured often in The New Testament as a defective and imperfect thing?

Though I have aimed to provide for a variety of affairs in the Christian life by the different metres, paraphrases, and divisions of the Psalms, of which I shall speak particularly, yet after all there are a great many circumstances that attend common Christians which cannot be agreeably expressed by any paraphrase on the words of David, and for these I have endeavoured to provide in my book of Hymns, that Christians might have something to sing in divine worship answerable to most or all their occasions. In the Preface to that book I have shewn the insufficiency of the common versions of the Psalms, and given further reasons for my present attempt.

I am not so vain as to expect that the few short hints I have mentioned in that Preface or in this should be sufficient to justify my performances in the judgment of all men, nor to convince and satisfy those who have long maintained different sentiments; all the favour therefore that I desire of my readers is this, that they would not censure this Work till they have read my

Difcourfe of Pfalmody, which I hope will fhortly be
publifhed; but let them read it with ferious attention,
and bring with them a generous and fincere foul, ready
to be convinced, and to receive truth wherefoever it
can be found. In that treatife I have given a large and
particular account how the Pfalms of Jewifh compofure ought to be tranflated for Chriftian worfhip, and
juftified the rules I lay down by fuch reafons as feem
to carry in them moft plentiful evidence and a fair
conviction.   :

If I might prefume fo much I would entreat them
alfo to forget their younger prejudices for a feafon, fo
far as to make a few experiments of thefe Songs, and
try whether they are not fuited through divine grace
to kindle in them a fire of zeal and love, and to exalt
the willing foul to an evangelick temper of joy and
praife; and if they fhall find by fweet experience any
devout affections raifed, and a holy frame of mind a-
wakened within them by thefe attempts of Chriftian
pfalmiftry, I perfuade myfelf that I fhall receive their
thanks, and be affifted by their prayers towards the
recovery of my health and my publick labours in the
church of Chrift. Whatfoever fentiments they had for-
merly entertained, yet furely they will not fuffer their
old and doubtful opinions to prevail againft their own
inward fenfations of piety and religious joy.   ·

Before I conclude I muft add a few things concern-

ing my divifion of the Pfalms, and my manner of ver-
fifying.

OF THE DIVISION OF THE PSALMS.

In many of thefe facred fongs it is evident that the
Pfalmift had feveral diftinct cafes in view at the fame
time, as Pfalm lxv. the firft four or five verfes defcribe
the temple-worfhip of prayer and praife, the following verfes reprefent the providence of God in the feafons of the year; fo in Pfalm lxviii. the firft fix verfes
declare the majefty and mercy of God, and from the
7th verfe to the 16th Ifrael is brought from Egypt to
fix divine worfhip at Jerufalem, the 17th and 18th
are a prophecy of the afcenfion of Chrift, ver. 24, &c,
defcribes a religious proceffion, &c. The like may be
obferved in many other Pfalms, efpecially fuch as reprefent fome complicated forrows or joys of the Pfalmift. Now it is not to be fuppofed that Chriftians fhould
have all the fame diftinct occafions of meditation, complaint, or praife, much lefs all at the fame time to be
mentioned before God, therefore I have divided many
Pfalms into feveral parts, and difpofed them into diftinct hymns on thofe various fubjects that may be proper matter for Chriftian pfalmody.

Befides that exceffive long tone of voice that ftretches
out every fyllable in our publick finging allows us neither time nor fpirits to fing above fix or eight ftanzas

D ij

his work will ever shine brightest among those that have confined themselves to a mere translation; but that close confinement has often forbid the freedom and glory of verse, and by cramping his sense has rendered it sometimes too obscure for a plain reader and the publick worship, even though we lived in the days of David and Judaism. These inconveniencies he himself suspects and fears in the Preface.

I am content to yield to Mr. Milbourne the preference of his poesy in several parts of his Psalms, and to Mr. Tate and Dr. Brady in some of theirs; but in those very places their turns of thought and language are too much raised above a vulgar audience, and fit only for persons of an higher education.

I have not refused in some few Psalms to borrow a single line or two from these three authors, yet I have taken the most freedom of that sort with Dr. Patrick, for his style best agrees with my design, though his verse be generally of a lower strain; but where I have used three or four lines together of any author I have acknowledged it in the Notes.

In some of the more elevated Psalms I have given a little indulgence to my genius; and if it should appear that I have aimed at the sublime, yet I have generally kept within the reach of an unlearned reader. I never thought the art of sublime writing consisted in flying out of sight, nor am I of the mind of the Italian who said, "Obscurity begets greatness." I have always avoided the language of the poets where it did not suit the language of the gospel.

In many of these compofures I have juſt permitted my verſe to rife above a flat and indolent ſtyle, yet I hope it is every where ſupported above the juſt contempt of the criticks, though I am ſenſible that I have often ſubdued it below their eſteem; becauſe I would neither indulge any bold metaphors, nor admit of hard words, nor tempt an ignorant worſhipper to ſing without his underſtanding.

'Though I have attempted to imitate the ſacred beauties of my author in ſome of the ſprightly Pſalms, ſuch as Pſalm xliv, xlvi, xlix, lxv, lxxii, xc, xci, civ, cxiv, cxv, cxxxix, &c. yet if my youthful readers complain that they expected to find here more elegant and beautiful deſcriptions, with which the ſacred original abounds, let them conſider that ſome of thoſe pieces of deſcriptive poeſy are the flowery elegancies peculiar to eaſtern nations and antique ages, and are much too large alſo to be brought into ſuch ſhort Chriſtian ſonnets as are uſed in our preſent worſhip; almoſt all thoſe Pſalms I have contracted and fitted to more ſpiritual devotion, as Pſalm xviii, lxviii, lxxiii, lxxviii, cv, cvi, cix, &c.

OF THE METRE AND RHYME.

I Have formed my verſe in the three moſt uſual metres to which our pſalm tunes are fitted, namely, the

Common Metre, the metre of the old xxvth Pfalm which I call Short Metre, and that of the old cdth Pfalm, which I call Long Metre. Befides thefe I have done fome few Pfalms in ftanzas of fix, eight, or twelve lines, to the beft of the old tunes; many of them I have alfo caft into two or three metres, not by leaving out or adding two fyllables in a line, whereby others have cramped or ftretched their verfe to the deftruction of all poefy, but I have made an entire new fong, and oftentimes in the different metres I have indulged thofe different fenfes in which commentators have explained the infpired author; and if in one metre I have given the loofe to a paraphrafe I have confined myfelf to my text in the other.

If I am charged by the criticks for repeating the fame rhymes too often, let them confider that the words which continually recur in divine poefy admit exceeding few rhymes to them fit for facred ufe, thefe are God, World, Flefh, Soul, Life, Death, Faith, Hope, Heaven, Earth, &c. which I think will make fufficient apology, efpecially fince I have coupled all my lines by rhymes much more than either Mr. Tate or Dr. Patrick have done, which is certainly moft mufical and agreeable to the ear where rhyme is ufed at all.

I muft confefs I have never yet feen any verfion or paraphrafe of the Pfalms, in their own Jewifh fenfe, so perfect as to discourage all further attempts; but whoever undertakes the noble work let him bring with him a soul devoted to piety, an exalted genius, and withal a studious application; for David's harp abhors a profane singer, and disdains to answer to an unskilful or a careless touch. A meaner pen may imitate at a distance, but a complete translation or a just paraphrase demands a rich treasury of diction and exalted fancy, a quick taste of devout passion, together with judgment strict and severe to retrench every luxuriant line, and to maintain a religious sovereignty over the whole work. Thus the Psalmist of Israel might arise in Great Britain in all his Hebrew glory, and entertain the more knowing and polite Christians of our age. But still I am bold to maintain the great principle on which my present Work is founded, and that is, that if the brightest genius on earth, or an angel from heaven, should translate David, and keep close to the sense and style of the inspired author, we should only obtain thereby a bright or heavenly copy of the devotions of the Jewish king; but it could never make the fittest psalmbook for a Christian people.

It was not my design to exalt myself to the rank and glory of poets, but I was ambitious to be a servant to the churches, and a helper to the joy of the meanest Christian. Though there are many gone before me who have taught the Hebrew Psalmist to speak Englifh, yet I think I may affume this pleafure, of being the firft who hath brought down the royal author into the common affairs of the Chriftian life, and led the Pfalmift of Ifrael into the church of Chrift, without any thing of a Jew about him: and whenfoever there fhall appear any paraphrafe of the book of Pfalms that retains more of the favour of David's piety, difcovers more of the ftyle and fpirit of the gofpel, with a fuperiour dignity of verfe, and yet the lines as eafy and flowing, and the fenfe and language as level to the loweft capacity, I fhall congratulate the world, and confent to fay, Let this attempt of mine be buried in filence.

Till fuch a work arife I muft attend thefe Evangelick Songs, which have been the labour of fo many years, with a devout wifh:

May that God who has favoured me with life and capacity to finifh this Work for the fervice of his churches, after fo many years of tirefome ficknefs and confinement, accept this humble offering from a thankful heart! May the Lord, who dwelt of old amidft the praifes of Ifrael, encourage and blefs this Effay to affift Chriftians in the work of praife! and may his churches exalt him here on earth in the language of his gofpel and his grace till they fhall be called up to heaven and the noble fociety above! there David and Afaph have changed their ancient ftyle, and the song of Moses and of the Lamb are one; there the Jews join with the nations to exalt their God and Redeemer in the language of angels, and in the strains of complete glory. Amen.

ADVERTISEMENT TO THE READERS.

The chief design of this Work was to improve Psalmody or religious singing, and to encourage the frequent practice of it in publick assemblies and private families with more honour and delight; yet the Author hopes the reading of it may also entertain in the parlour and the closet with devout pleasure and holy meditations; therefore he would request his readers at proper seasons to peruse it thorough, and among three hundred and forty sacred Hymns they may find out several that suit their own case and temper, or the circumstances of their families and friends; they may teach their children such as are proper for their age, and by treasuring them in their memory they may be furnished for pious retirement, or may entertain their friends with holy melody.

OF CHUSING OR FINDING THE PSALM.

The perusal of the whole book will acquaint every reader with the Author's method, and by consulting the Index or Table of Contents he may find hymns very proper for many occasions of the Christian life and worship, though no copy of David's Psalter can provide for all.

Or if he remember the first line of any Psalm, the Table of the first Lines will direct where to find it.

Or if any shall think it best to sing all the Psalms in order in churches or families, it may be done with profit, provided those Psalms be omitted that refer to special occurrences of nations, churches, or single Christians.

OF NAMING THE PSALM.

Let the number of the Psalm be named distinctly, together with the particular metre, and particular part of it; as for instance, *Let us sing the 33d Psalm, 2d Part, Common Metre;* or, *Let us sing the 91st Psalm, 1st Part, beginning at the Pause,* or, *ending at the Pause;* or, *Let us sing the 84th Psalm as the 148th Psalm,* &c. and then read over the first stanza before you begin to sing, that the people may find it in their books, whether you sing with or without reading line by line.

OF DIVIDING THE PSALM.

If the Psalm be too long for the time or custom of singing, there are Pauses in many of them at which you may properly rest; or you may leave out those

verfes which are included in crotchets [ ] without di-
fturbing the fenfe; or in fome places you may begin
to fing at a Paufe.

Do not always cònfine yourfelves to fix ftanzas, but
fing feven or eight rather than confound the fenfe,
and abufe the Pfalm in folemn worfhip.

OF THE MANNER OF SINGING.

It were to be wifhed that all congregations and private families would fing as they do in foreign Proteftant countries, without reading line by line. Though
the Author has done what he could to make the fenfe
complete in every line or two, yet many inconveniencies will always attend this unhappy manner of
finging; but where it cannot be altered thefe two
things may give fome relief.

Firft, Let as many as can do it bring pfalmbooks
with them, and look on the words while they fing, fo
far as to make the fenfe complete.

Secondly, Let the Clerk read the whole Pfalm over
aloud before he begins to parcel out the lines, that the
people may have fome notion of what they fing, and
not be forced to drag on heavily through eight tedious fyllables without any meaning till the next line
comes to give the fenfe of them.

2

It were to be wished also that we might not dwell
so long upon every single note, and produce the syl-
lables to such a tiresome extent, with a constant uni-
formity of time, which disgraces the musick, and puts
the congregation quite out of breath in singing five
or six stanzas; whereas if the method of singing were
but reformed to a greater speed in pronunciation we
might often enjoy the pleasure of a longer Psalm with
less expense of time and breath, and our psalmody
would be more agreeable to that of the ancient churches, more intelligible to others, and more delightful to
ourselves.

    Dec. 1. 1718.

---

*The various Measures of the Verse are fitted to the Tunes
of the Old Psalmbook.*

    To the Common Tunes sing all intitled *Common
Metre.*

    To the Tunes of the 100dth Psalm sing all intitled
Long Metre.

    To the Tune of the 25th Psalm sing *Short Metre.*

    To the 50th Psalm sing one Metre of the 50th, 93d.

    To the 112th or 127th Psalm sing one Metre of the
104th and 148th.

    To the 113th Psalm sing one Metre of the 19th,
33d, 58th, 89th, last Part, 96th, 112th, 113th.

To the 122d Pfalm fing one of the Metres of the 93d, 122d, and 133d.

To the 148th Pfalm fing one Metre of the 84th, 121ft, 136th, and 148th.

To a New Tune fing one Metre of the 50th and 115th.

PSALM I. Common Metre.

The way and end of the righteous and the wicked.

BLESS'D is the man who shuns the place
Where sinners love to meet,
Who fears to tread their wicked ways,
And hates the scoffer's seat;   4

  2. But in the statutes of the Lord
Has plac'd his chief delight;
By day he reads or hears the Word,
And meditates by night.   8

  [3. He, like a plant of gen'rous kind
By living waters set,
Safe from the storms and blasting wind
Enjoys a peaceful state.]   12

  4. Green as the leaf and ever fair
Shall his profession shine,
While fruits of holiness appear
Like clusters on the vine.   16

  5. Not so th' impious and unjust;
What vain designs they form!
Their hopes are blown away like dust
Or chaff before the storm.   20

6. Sinners in judgment shall not stand
Amongst the sons of grace,
When Christ the Judge at his right hand
Appoints his saints a place.   24

7. His eye beholds the path they tread,
His heart approves it well,
But crooked ways of sinners lead
Down to the gates of hell *.   28

PSALM I. Short Metre.

The saint happy, the sinner miserable.

THE man is ever bless'd
Who shuns the sinner's ways,
Among their councils never stands,
Nor takes the scorner's place,   4

2. But makes the law of God
His study and delight
Amidst the labours of the day
And watches of the night.   8

3. He like a tree shall thrive
With waters near the root :
Fresh as the leaf his name shall live ;
His works are heav'nly fruit.   12

* In this Work I have often borrowed a line or two from The
New Testament, that the excellent and inspired composures of
the Jewish Psalmist may be brightened by the clearer discove-
ries of the Gospel.—Stanza vi. *He shall set the sheep at his right
hand, &c.* Matt. xxv. 33.

4. Not so th' ungodly race;
They no such blessings find:
Their hopes shall fly like empty chaff
Before the driving wind.   16

5. How will they bear to stand
Before that judgment-seat
Where all the saints at Christ's right hand
In full assembly meet?   20

6. He knows and he approves
The way the righteous go,
But sinners and their works shall meet
A dreadful overthrow.   24

PSALM I. Long Metre.

The difference between the righteous and the wicked.

HAPPY the man whose cautious feet
Shun the broad way that sinners go,
Who hates the place where Atheists meet,
And fears to talk as scoffers do.   4

2. He loves t' employ his morning-light
Amongst the statutes of the Lord,
And spends the wakeful hours of night
With pleasure, pond'ring o'er the Word.   8

3. He like a plant by gentle streams
Shall flourish in immortal green,
And Heav'n will shine with kindest beams
On ev'ry work his hands begin.   12

4. But sinners find their counsels cross'd:
As chaff before the tempest flies,
So shall their hopes be blown and lost
When the last trumpet shakes the skies.   16

5. In vain the rebel seeks to stand
In judgment with the pious race,
The dreadful Judge with stern command
Divides him to a diff'rent place.   20

6. " Straight is the way my saints have trod,
" I bless'd the path and drew it plain,
" But you would chuse the crooked road,
" And down it leads to endless pain †."   24

PSALM II. Short Metre.

Translat. according to the divine pattern, Ac. iv. 24, &c.

Christ dying, rising, interceding, and reigning.

[MAKER and sov'reign Lord
Of heav'n, and earth, and seas,
Thy providence confirms thy word
And answers thy decrees.   4

2. The things so long foretold
By David are fulfill'd,
When Jews and Gentiles join to slay
Jesus thine holy child.]   8

† Stanza i. line 2. and stanza vi. line 4. *Bread is the way
that leads to destruction,* Matt. vii. 13. 14.---Stanza iv. line 4.
As the last trump, &c. 1 Cor. xv. 52.

3. Why did the Gentiles rage,
And Jews with one accord
Bend all their counfels to deftroy
Th' Anointed of the Lord? 12

4. Rulers and kings agree
To form a vain defign;
Againft the Lord their pow'rs unite,
Againft his Chrift they join. 16

5. The Lord derides their rage,
And will fupport his throne;
He that hath rais'd him from the dead
Hath own'd him for his Son. 20

PAUSE.

6. Now he 's afcended high,
And afks to rule the earth,
The merit of his blood he pleads,
And pleads his heav'nly birth. 24

7. He afks, and God beftows
A large inheritance;
Far as the world's remoteft ends
His kingdom fhall advance. 28

8. The nations that rebel
Muft feel his iron rod;
He 'll vindicate thofe honours well
Which he receiv'd from God. 32

[9. Be wife, ye Rulers! now,
And worfhip at his throne;
With trembling joy ye People! bow
To God's exalted Son. 36

10. If once his wrath arife
Ye perifh on the place;
Then bleffed is the foul that flies
For refuge to his grace †.]   40

PSALM II. Common Metre.

Why did the nations join to flay
The Lord's anointed Son?
Why did they caft his laws away
And tread his gofpel down?   .   4

   2. The Lord that fits above the fkies
Derides their rage below,
He fpeaks with vengeance in his eyes
And ftrikes their fpirits thro'.   8

   3. " I call him my Eternal Son,
" And raife him from the dead;
" I make my holy hill his throne,
" And wide his kingdom fpread.   12

   4. " Afk me, my Son, and then enjoy
" The utmoft Heathen lands:
" Thy rod of iron fhall deftroy
" The rebel that withftands."   16

† Stanza i. line 1. *Lord, thou art God who haft made Heaven
—Who by the mouth of thy fervant David haft faid, Why did the
Heathen rage, &c.* Acts iv. 24, &c.——Stanza i. line 3. *To do
whatfoever thy hand and thy counfel determined to be done,* &c.
ver. 28. And feveral other lines of this verfion are evidently
borrowed from the fuller difcoveries of Chrift in The New
Teftament.——Stanza viii. *Shall rule the nations with a rod
of iron, even as I received of my Father,* Rev. ii. 27.

5. Be wife ye Rulers of the earth,
Obey th' anointed Lord,
Adore the King of heav'nly birth,
And tremble at his word.   20

6. With humble love addrefs his throne,
For if ye frown ye die:
Thofe are fecure and thofe alone
Who on his grace rely.   24

PSALM II. Long Metre.

Chrift's death, refurrection, and afcenfion.

Why did the Jews proclaim their rage?
The Romans why their fwords employ
Againft the Lord? their pow'rs engage
His dear Anointed to deftroy?   4

2. "Come, let us break his bands," they fay,
"This man fhall never give us laws:"
And thus they caft his yoke away,
And nail'd the Monarch to the crofs.   8

3. But God, who high in glory reigns,
Laughs at their pride, their rage controls;
He 'll vex their hearts with inward pains,
And fpeak in thunder to their fouls.   12

4. "I will maintain the King I made
"On Zion's everlafting hill;
"My hand fhall bring him from the dead,
"And he fhall ftand your Sov'reign ftill." 16

[5. His wondrous rifing from the earth
Makes his eternal Godhead known :
The Lord declares his heav'nly birth,
" This day have I begot my Son.   20

   6. " Afcend my Son to my right hand,
" There thou fhalt afk and I beftow
" The utmoft bounds of Heathen land;
" To thee the northern ifles fhall bow."]   24

   7. But nations that refift his grace
Shall fall before his iron ftroke :
His rod fhall crufh his foes with eafe,
As potters' earthen work is broke.   28

PAUSE.

   8. Now ye that fit on earthly thrones
Be wife, and ferve the Lord, the Lamb;
Now at his feet fubmit your crowns,
Rejoice and tremble at his name.   32

   9. With humble love addrefs the Son,
Left he grow angry and ye die :
His wrath will burn to worlds unknown
If ye provoke his jealoufy.   36

   10. His ftorms fhall drive you quick to hell;
He is a God, and ye but duft :
Happy the fouls that know him well,
And make his grace their only truft *.   40

   * Stanza v. *Declared to be the Son of God with power by his
refurrection from the dead*, Rom. i. 4.

PSALM III. Common Metre.

*Doubts and fears suppressed, or, God our defence from sin
and Satan.*

My God, how many are my fears!
How fast my foes increase!
Conspiring my eternal death
They break my present peace.   4

2. The lying tempter would persuade
There's no relief in Heav'n,
And all my swelling sins appear
Too big to be forgiv'n.   8

3. But thou, my glory and my strength,
Shalt on the tempter tread,
Shalt silence all my threat'ning guilt,
And raise my drooping head.   12

[4. I cry'd, and from his holy hill
He bow'd a list'ning ear:
I call'd my Father and my God,
And he subdu'd my fear.   16

5. He shed soft slumbers on mine eyes
In spite of all my foes:
I 'woke, and wonder'd at the grace
That guarded my repose.]   20

6. What tho' the hosts of Death and Hell
All arm'd against me stood?
Terrours no more shall shake my soul;
My refuge is my God.   24

7. Arife O Lord! fulfil thy grace
While I thy glory fing :
My God has broke the ferpent's teeth,
And Death has loft his fting.   28

8. Salvation to the Lord belongs,
His arm alone can fave ;
Bleffings attend thy people here,
And reach beyond the grave †.   32

PSALM III. ver. 1, 2, 3, 4, 5, 8. Long Metre.

A morning Pfalm.

O Lord, how many are my foes
In this weak ftate of flefh and blood !
My peace they daily difcompofe,
But my defence and hope is God.   4

2. Tir'd with the burdens of the day
To thee I rais'd an ev'ning cry :
Thou heard'ft when I began to pray,
And thine almighty help was nigh.   8

3. Supported by thine heav'nly aid
I laid me down and flept fecure :
Not death fhould make my heart afraid
Tho' I fhould wake and rife no more.   12

† In this Pfalm I have changed David's perfonal enemies into
the fpiritual enemies of every Chriftian, namely, fin, Satan, &c.
and have mentioned the ferpent, the tempter, the guilt of fin,
and the fting of death, which are words well known in The
New Teftament.

4. But God fuftain'd me all the night;
Salvation doth to God belong;
He rais'd my head to fee the light,
And make his praife my morning fong †. 16

PSALM IV. ver. 1, 2, 3, 5, 6, 7. Long Metre.

Hearing of prayer, or, *God our portion, and Chrift our hope.*

O God of grace and righteoufnefs
Hear and attend when I complain;
Thou haft enlarg'd me in diftrefs,
Bow down a gracious ear again. 4

2. Ye Sons of men! in vain ye try
To turn my glory into fhame:
How long will fcoffers love to lie
And dare reproach my Saviour's name? 8

3. Know that the Lord divides his faints
From all the tribes of men befide;
He hears the cry of penitents
For the dear fake of Chrift that dy'd. 12

4. When our obedient hands have done
A thoufand works of righteoufnefs
We put our truft in God alone,
And glory in his pard'ning grace. 16

† In the 3d and 4th Pfalms there is a verfe or two that fhew
the one to be writ in the morning the other in the evening,
wherefore I have chofen out thofe parts that feem moft eafily
applicable, and have turned them into a morning and evening
fong.

5. Let the unthinking many say
" Who will beftow fome earthly good?"
But Lord, thy light and love we pray;
Our fouls defire this heav'nly food.   20

6. Then fhall my cheerful pow'rs rejoice
At grace and favour fo divine,
Nor will I change my happy choice
For all their corn and all their wine †.   24

PSALM IV. ver. 3, 4, 5, 8. Common Metre.

An evening Pfalm.

Lord, thou wilt hear me when I pray;
I am for ever thine;
I fear before thee all the day,
Nor would I dare to fin.   4

2. And while I reft my weary head,
From cares and bus'nefs free,
'Tis fweet converfing on my bed
With my own heart and thee.   8

3. I pay this ev'ning facrifice;
And when my work is done,
Great God! my faith and hope relies
Upon thy grace alone.   12

† Though this Pfalm may not directly intend the Meffiah, yet
I have taken occafion to apply fome expreffions in it to Chrift
and his gofpel, I hope with fome advantage, and without offence.

4. Thus with my thoughts compos'd to peace
I'll give my eyes to sleep;
Thy hand in safety keeps my days
And will my slumbers keep.   16

PSALM V. Common Metre.

For the Lord's day morning.

Lord, in the morning thou shalt hear
My voice ascending high;
To thee will I direct my pray'r,
To thee lift up mine eye,   4

2. Up to the hills where Christ is gone
To plead for all his saints,
Presenting at his Father's throne
Our songs and our complaints.   8

3. Thou art a God before whose sight
The wicked shall not stand;
Sinners shall ne'er be thy delight,
Nor dwell at thy right hand.   12

4. But to thy house will I resort
To taste thy mercies there;
I will frequent thine holy court,
And worship in thy fear.   16

5. O may thy spirit guide my feet
In ways of righteousness,
Make ev'ry path of duty straight
And plain before my face!   20

PAUSE.

6. My watchful enemies combine
To tempt my feet aftray;
They flatter with a bafe defign
To make my foul their prey. 24

7. Lord, crufh the ferpent in the duft,
And all his plots deftroy;
While thofe that in thy mercy truft
For ever fhout for joy. 28

8. The men that love and fear thy name
Shall fee their hopes fulfill'd;
The mighty God will compafs them
With favour as a fhield *. 32

PSALM VI. Common Metre.

Complaint in ficknefs, or, Difeafes healed.

In anger Lord rebuke me not,
Withdraw the dreadful ftorm;
Nor let thy fury grow fo hot
Againft a feeble worm. 4

* This Pfalm begins with the mention of morning prayer, and proceeds to the worfhip of God in his temple, which inclined me to entitle it, *for a Lord's day morning.*-----Stanza ii. and v. Where any juft occafion is given to make mention of Chrift and the Holy Spirit I refufe it not, and I am perfuaded David would not have refufed it had he lived under the gofpel, nor St. Paul, had he written a pfalmbook.

2. My soul 's bow'd down with heavy cares,
My flesh with pain oppreft;
My couch is witnefs to my tears,
My tears forbid my reft.   8

   3. Sorrow and pain wear out my days,
I wafte the night with cries,
Counting the minutes as they pafs
Till the flow morning rife.   12

   4. Shall I be ftill tormented more,
Mine eye confum'd with grief?
How long my God, how long before
Thy hand afford relief?   16

   5. He hears when duft and afhes fpeak,
He pities all our groans,
He faves us for his mercy's fake,
And heals our broken bones.   20

   6. The virtue of his fov'reign word
Reftores our fainting breath;
For filent graves praife not the Lord,
Nor is he known in death *.   24

---

* Vexation by perfonal enemies is not a conftant attendant of
ficknefs, therefore in this verfion I have omitted it as a peculiar circumftance of David's: In the next verfion I have changed thefe enemies for temptations and defpairing thoughts.——
The vth ftanza of this Pfalm, which is a plea in the prayer, may
be naturally tranfpofed to the end as a ground of praife.

PSALM VI. Long Metre.

Temptations in sickness overcome.

LORD, I can suffer thy rebukes
When thou with kindness dost chastise,
But thy fierce wrath I cannot bear,
O let it not against me rise!   4

  2. Pity my languishing estate,
And ease the sorrows that I feel;
The wounds thine heavy hand hath made
O let thy gentler touches heal!   8

  3. See how I pass my weary days
In sighs and groans, and when 't is night
My bed is water'd with my tears;
My grief consumes and dims my sight.   12

  4. Look how the pow'rs of Nature mourn!
How long almighty God! how long?
When shall thine hour of grace return?
When shall I make thy grace my song?   16

  5. I feel my flesh so near the grave
My thoughts are tempted to despair;
But graves can never praise the Lord,
For all is dull and silence there.   20

  6. Depart ye Tempters! from my soul,
And all despairing thoughts depart:
My God who hears my humble moan
Will ease my flesh and cheer my heart†.   24

† Part of the three first stanzas I have borrowed from Dr. Patrick, being pleased with the agreeable turn he gives to David's sense.

PSALM VII. Common Metre.

God's care of his people, and punishment of persecutors.

My truft is in my heav'nly Friend,
My hope in thee my God;
Rife and my helplefs life defend
From thofe that feek my blood.   4

   2. With infolence and fury they
My foul in pieces tear,
As hungry lions rend the prey
When no deliv'rer 's near.   8

   3. If I had e'er provok'd them firft
Or once abus'd my foe,
Then let him tread my life to duft
And lay mine honour low.   12

   4. If there be malice hid in me,
I know thy piercing eyes,
I fhould not dare appeal to thee,
Nor afk my God to rife.   16

   5. Arife my God, lift up thy hand,
Their pride and pow'r control;
Awake to judgment, and command
Deliv'rance for my foul.   20

PAUSE.

   6. Let finners and their wicked rage
Be humbled to the duft :
Shall not the God of truth engage
To vindicate the juft ?   24

7. He knows the heart, he tries the reins,
He will defend th' upright;
His fharpeft arrows he ordains
Againſt the fons of fpite.   28

8. For me their malice digg'd a pit,
But there themſelves are caſt;
My God makes all their miſchief light
On their own heads at laſt.   32

9. That cruel perſecuting race
Muſt feel his dreadful ſword.
Awake my Soul! and praiſe the grace
And juſtice of the Lord *.   36

PSALM VIII. Short Metre.

*God's ſovereignty and goodneſs, and man's dominion over
the creatures.*

O Lord, our heav'nly King,
Thy name is all divine,
Thy glories round the earth are ſpread,
And o'er the heav'ns they ſhine.   4

2. When to thy works on high
I raiſe my wond'ring eyes,
And ſee the moon complete in light
Adorn the darkſome ſkies;   8

* In this Pſalm I have not exactly followed every ſingle verſe
of the Pſalmiſt, but have endeavoured to contract the ſubſtance
of it into fewer lines, yet not without a regard to the literal
ſenſe and words alfo, as will appear by the comparifon.

3. When I survey the stars
And all their shining forms,
Lord what is man, that worthless thing,
Akin to dust and worms? 12

4. Lord what is worthless man
That thou shouldst love him so?
Next to thine angels is he plac'd,
And lord of all below. 16

5. Thine honours crown his head
While beasts like slaves obey,
And birds that cut the air with wings
And fish that cleave the sea. 20

6. How rich thy beunties are!
And wondrous are thy ways!
Of dust and worms thy pow'r can frame
A monument of praise. 24

[7. Out of the mouths of babes
And sucklings thou canst draw
Surprising honours to thy name,
And strike the world with awe. 28

8. O Lord our heav'nly King
Thy name is all divine;
Thy glories round the earth are spread,
And o'er the heav'ns they shine *. 32

† Stanza vii. The transposing of the 2d verse of this Psalm
towards the end will not appear offensive, since the connexion
of it with the other parts of the Psalm appears so much more
visible.

PSALM VIII. Common Metre.

Chrift's condefcenfion and glorification, or, *God made man.*

O Lord our Lord, how wondrous great
Is thine exalted name!
The glories of thy heav'nly ftate
Let men and babes proclaim.   4

  2. When I behold thy works on high,
The moon that rules the night,
And ftars that well adorn the fky,
Thofe moving worlds of light;   8

  3. Lord! what is man, or all his race,
Who dwells fo far below,
That thou fhouldft vifit him with grace,
And love his nature fo?   12

  4. That thine Eternal Son fhould bear
To take a mortal form,
Made lower than his angels are,
To fave a dying worm?   16

  [5. Yet while he liv'd on earth unknown,
And men would not adore,
Th' obedient feas and fifhes own
His godhead and his pow'r.   20

  6. The waves lay fpread beneath his feet,
And fifh at his command
Bring their large fhoals to Peter's net,
Bring tribute to his hand.   24

7. Thefe leffer glories of the Son
Shone thro' the flefhly cloud;
Now we behold him on his throne,
And men confefs him God.] 28

8. Let him be crown'd with majefty
Who bow'd his head to death,
And be his honours founded high
By all things that have breath. 32

9. Jefus our Lord, how wondrous great
Is thine exalted name!
The glories of thy heav'nly ftate
Let the whole earth proclaim †. 36

PSALM VIII. ver. 1, 2. paraphrafed. The firft part.
Long Metre.

The Hofanna of the children, or, *Infants praifing God.*

ALMIGHTY Ruler of the fkies,
Thro' the wide earth thy name is fpread,
And thine eternal glories rife
O'er all the heav'ns thy hands have made. 4

† Stan. iv. If the citation of part of this Pfalm by the apoftle,
Heb. ii. 5. be but a mere allufion, yet it affords ground enough
for the turn I have given it in this verfion, and the application
of it to Chrift.—Stanza vi. line 1. *Jefus went to them walking
on the fea*, Matt. xiv. 25.———Line 2. *He faid to Simon, Launch
out, &c. and they enclofed a great multitude of fifhes*, Luke v.
4, 6.—Line 4. *Caft an hook and take up the fifh —thou fhalt find
piece of money, &c.* Matt. xvii. 27.

2. To thee the voices of the young
A monument of honour raise,
And babes with uninstructed tongue
Declare the wonders of thy praise.   8

3. Thy pow'r assists their tender age
To bring proud rebels to the ground,
To still the bold blasphemer's rage,
And all their policies confound.   12

4. Children amidst thy temple throng
To see their great Redeemer's face;
The Son of David is their song,
And young hosannas fill the place.   16

5. The frowning scribes and angry priests
In vain their impious cavils bring;
Revenge sits silent in their breasts
Whilst Jewish babes proclaim their King *.   20

PSALM VIII. ver. 3, &c. paraphrased. The second part.
Long Metre.

Adam and Christ lords of the old and the new creation.

LORD, what was man when made at first,
Adam the offspring of the dust,
That thou shouldst set him and his race
But just below an angel's place ?   4

* The two first verses are here paraphrased, and explained by
the history of the children crying Hosanna to Christ, *Matt.* xxi.
15, 16. where our Saviour cites and applies those words of the
Psalmist.

I

2. That thou shouldst raise his nature so,
And make him lord of all below,
Make ev'ry beast and bird submit,
And lay the fishes at his feet ? 8

3. But O! what brighter glories wait
To crown the second Adam's state!
What honours shall thy Son adorn
Who condescended to be born! 12

4. See him below his angels made,
See him in dust amongst the dead,
To save a ruin'd world from sin;
But he shall reign with pow'r divine. 16

5. The world to come, redeem'd from all
The mis'ries that attend the fall,
New made and glorious, shall submit
At our exalted Saviour's feet ‡. 20

PSALM IX. The first part.

Wrath and mercy from the judgment-seat.

WITH my whole heart I 'll raise my song,
Thy wonders I 'll proclaim;
Thou sov'reign Judge of right and wrong
Wilt put my foes to shame. 4

‡ I am persuaded the true meaning of the apostle in citing the
words of this Psalm, and applying them to our Saviour, *Heb.*
ii. 5. &c. is to shew that Christ the second Adam must have
dominion over the new world, as Adam the first man had
over the old, and that he is truly and really man, because the
first Adam is the figure and type of him in this his dominion.

2. I 'll fing thy majefty and grace;
My God prepares his throne
To judge the world in righteoufnefs,
And make his vengeance known.   8

3. Then fhall the Lord a refuge prove
For all the poor oppreft,
To fave the people of his love
And give the weary reft.   12

4. The men that know thy name will truft
In thy abundant grace,
For thou haft ne'er forfook the juft
Who humbly feek thy face.   16

5. Sing praifes to the righteous Lord
Who dwells on Zion's hill,
Who executes his threat'ning word,
And doth his grace fulfil.   20

PSALM IX. ver. 12. The fecond part.

The wifdom and equity of Providence.

WHEN the great Judge, fupreme and juft,
Shall once inquire for blood,
The humble fouls that mourn in duft
Shall find a faithful God.   4

2. He from the dreadful gates of death
Does his own children raife;
In Zion's gates with cheerful breath
They fing their Father's praife.   8

3. His foes shall fall with heedless feet
Into the pit they made,
And sinners perish in the net
That their own hands have spread.　　　　12

4. Thus by thy judgments mighty God!
Are thy deep counsels known:
When men of mischief are destroy'd
The snare must be their own.　　　　16

PAUSE.

5. The wicked shall sink down to hell:
Thy wrath devours the lands
That dare forget thee, or rebel
Against thy known commands.　　　　20

6. Tho' saints to sore distress are brought,
And wait and long complain,
Their cries shall not be still forgot,
Nor shall their hopes be vain.　　　　24

[7. Rise great Redeemer! from thy seat
To judge and save the poor,
Let nations tremble at thy feet,
And man prevail no more.　　　　28

8. Thy thunder shall affright the proud
And put their hearts to pain,
Make them confess that thou art God
And they but feeble men.]　　　　32

G ij

PSALM X.

Prayer heard, and saints saved, or, *Pride, Atheism, and oppression, punished.*

For a humiliation day.

Why doth the Lord stand off so far,
And why conceal his face,
When great calamities appear
And times of deep distress?   4

  2. Lord, shall the wicked still deride
Thy justice and thy pow'r?
Shall they advance their heads in pride
And still thy saints devour?   8

  3. They put thy judgments from their sight
And then insult the poor;
They boast in their exalted height
That they shall fall no more.   12

  4. Arise O God! lift up thine hand,
Attend our humble cry;
No enemy shall dare to stand
When God ascends on high.   16

PAUSE.

  5. Why do the men of malice rage,
And say with foolish pride
" The God of heav'n will ne'er engage
" To fight on Zion's side."   13

6. But thou for ever art our Lord,
And pow'rful is thine hand,
As when the Heathens felt thy fword,
And perifh'd from thy land. R 4

7. Thou wilt prepare our hearts to pray,
And caufe thine ear to hear;
He hearkens what his children fay,
And puts the world in fear. 28

8. Proud tyrants fhall no more opprefs,
No more defpife the juft,
And mighty finners fhall confefs
They are but earth and duft. 32

PSALM XI.

God loves the righteous and hates the wicked.

My refuge is the God of love;
Why do my foes infult and cry,
" Fly like a tim'rous trembling dove,
" To diftant woods or mountains fly?" 4

2. If government be all deftroy'd,
(That firm foundation of our peace)
And violence make juftice void,
Where fhall the righteous feek redrefs? 8

3. The Lord in heav'n has fix'd his throne,
His eye furveys the world below;
To him all mortal things are known,
His eyelids fearch our fpirits thro'. 12

G iij

4. If he afflicts his faints fo far
To prove their love and try their grace,
What may the bold tranfgreffors fear!
His very foul abhors their ways.   16

   5 On impious wretches he fhall rain
Tempefts of brimftone, fire, and death,
Such as he kindled on the plain
Of Sodom with his angry breath.   20

   6. The righteous Lord loves righteous fouls,
Whofe thoughts and actions are fincere,
And with a gracious eye beholds
The men that his own image bear.   24

PSALM XII. Long Metre.

The faints' fafety and hope in evil times, or, Sins of the
tongue complained of, viz. blafphemy, falfehood, &c.

LORD, if thou doft not foon appear
Virtue and truth will fly away;
A faithful man amongft us here
Will fcarce be found if thou delay.   4

   2. The whole difcourfe when neighbours meet
Is fill'd with trifles loofe and vain;
Their lips are flatt'ry and deceit,
And their proud language is profane.   8

   3. But lips that with deceit abound
Shall not maintain their triumph long;
The God of vengeance will confound
The flatt'ring and blafpheming tongue.   12

4. " Yet fhall our words be free," they cry;
" Our tongue fhall be controll'd by none:
" Where is the lord will afk us why,
" Or fay our lips are not our own?" 16

5. The Lord who fees the poor oppreft,
And hears th' oppreffor's haughty ftrain,
Will rife to give his children reft,
Nor fhall they truft his word in vain. 20

6. Thy word O Lord! tho' often try'd,
Void of deceit fhall ftill appear;
Not filver feven times purify'd
From drofs and mixture fhines fo clear. 24

7. Thy grace fhall in the darkeft hour
Defend the holy foul from harm;
Tho' when the vileft men have pow'r
On ev'ry fide will finners fwarm. 28

PSALM XII. Common Metre.

Complaint of a general corruption of manners, or, The pro-
mife and fign of Chrift's coming to judgment.

HELP Lord! for men of virtue fail,
Religion lofes ground,
The fons of violence prevail,
And treacheries abound. 4

2. Their oaths and promifes they break,
Yet act the flatt'rer's part;
With fair deceitful lips they fpeak,
And with a double heart. 8

3. If we reprove some hateful lie
How is their fury stirr'd!
" Are not our lips our own," they cry,
" And who shall be our lord?"　　　　　　12

4. Scoffers appear on ev'ry side,
Where a vile race of men
Is rais'd to seats of pow'r and pride,
And bears the sword in vain.　　　　　　16

PAUSE.

5. Lord! when iniquities abound,
And blasphemy grows bold,
When faith is hardly to be found,
And love is waxing cold,　　　　　　20

6. Is not thy chariot hast'ning on?
Hast thou not giv'n the sign?
May we not trust and live upon
A promise so divine?　　　　　　24

7. " Yes," saith the Lord, " now will I rise
" And make oppressors flee;
" I shall appear to their surprise,
" And set my servants free."　　　　　　28

8. Thy word like silver sev'n times try'd
Thro' ages shall endure;
The men that in thy truth confide
Shall find the promise sure †.　　　　　　32

† Stanza iv. The last verse of this Psalm may naturally be inserted here.—Stanza v. The signs of Christ's coming mentioned in The New Testament, *Matt.* xxiv. 12. *Luke* xviii. 8. are
abounding iniquity, love waxing cold, and faith scarce to be
found, and seem very much akin to the sense of this Psalm.

PSALM XIII. Long Metre.

Pleading with God under defertion, or, Hope in darkness.

How long O Lord fhall I complain,
Like one that feeks his God in vain?
Canft thou thy face for ever hide,
And I ftill pray and be deny'd? 4

   2. Shall I for ever be forgot
As one whom thou regardeft not?
Still fhall my foul thine abfence mourn,
And ftill defpair of thy return? 8

   3. How long fhall my poor troubled breaft
Be with thefe anxious thoughts oppreft,
And Satan my malicious foe
Rejoice to fee me funk fo low? 12

   4. Hear Lord, and grant me quick relief
Before my death conclude my grief:
If thou withhold thy heav'nly light
I fleep in everlafting night. 16

   5. How will the pow'rs of darknefs boaft
If but one praying foul be loft?
But I have trufted in thy grace,
And fhall again behold thy face. 20

   6. Whate'er my fears or foes fuggeft
Thou art my hope, my joy, my reft:
My heart fhall feel thy love, and raife
My cheerful voice to fongs of praife. 24

PSALM XIII. Common Metre.

Complaint under temptations of the devil.

How long wilt thou conceal thy face,
My God, how long delay?
When shall I feel those heav'nly rays
That chase my fears away?   4

2. How long shall my poor lab'ring soul
Wrestle and toil in vain?
Thy word can all my foes control
And ease my raging pain.   8

3. See how the prince of darkness tries
All his malicious arts;
He spreads a mist around my eyes,
And throws his fiery darts.   12

4. Be thou my sun, and thou my shield,
My soul in safety keep;
Make haste, before mine eyes are seal'd
In death's eternal sleep.   16

5. How would the tempter boast aloud
If I become his prey!
Behold the sons of hell grow proud
At thy so long delay.   20

6. But they shall fly at thy rebuke,
And Satan hide his head;
He knows the terrours of thy look,
And hears thy voice with dread.   24

7. Thou wilt difplay that fov'reign grace
Where all my hopes have hung :
I fhall employ my lips in praife,
And vict'ry fhall be fung.   28

PSALM XIV. Firft part.

By nature all men are finners.

Fools in their heart believe and fay
" That all religion 's vain,
" There is no God that reigns on high   .
" Or minds th' affairs of men."   4
   2. From thoughts fo dreadful and profane
Corrupt difcourfe proceeds,
And in their impious hands are found
Abominable deeds.   8
   3. The Lord from his celeftial throne
Look'd down on things below,
To find the man that fought his grace
Or did his juftice know.   12
   4. By nature all are gone aftray,
Their practice all the fame ;
There 's none that fears his Maker's hand,
There 's none that loves his name.   16
   5. Their tongues are us'd to fpeak deceit,
Their flanders never ceafe ;
How fwift to mifchief are their feet !
Nor know the paths of peace.   20

6. Such feeds of fin (that bitter root)
In ev'ry heart are found,
Nor can they bear diviner fruit
Till grace refine the ground ‡.   24

PSALM. XIV. Second part.

The folly of perfecutors.

ARE finners now fo fenfelefs grown
That they the faints devour,
And never worfhip at thy throne,
Nor fear thine awful pow'r?   4

ɩ 2. Great God! appear to their furprife,
Reveal thy dreadful name;
Let them no more thy wrath defpife,
Nor turn our hope to fhame.   8

3. Doft thou not dwell among the juft?
And yet our foes deride
That we fhould make thy name our truft;
Great God! confound their pride.   12

4. O that the joyful day were come
To finifh our diftrefs!
When God fhall bring his children home,
Our fongs fhall never ceafe.   16

‡ Several verfes of this Pfalm are cited by the apoftle, *Rom.* iii. 10, &c. to fhew the univerfal corruption of human nature, wherefore I have brought more of the apoftle's words there ufed into the ivth and vth ftanzas here, and concluded this part of the Pfalm agreeably to St. Paul's defign.—*Note,* The 2d part of this Pfalm fpeaks only of perfecutors and the enemies of the church, therefore I have divided it from the former.

4

PSALM XV. Common Metre.

Characters of a saint, or a citizen of Zion, or, *The qualifications of a Christian.*

Who shall inhabit in thy hill
O God of holiness?
Whom will the Lord admit to dwell
So near his throne of grace ?　　　　　　　　4

2. The man that walks in pious ways
And works with righteous hands,
That trusts his Maker's promises
And follows his commands.　　　　　　　　8

3. He speaks the meaning of his heart,
Nor slanders with his tongue,
Will scarce believe an ill report,
Nor do his neighbour wrong.　　　　　　　12

4. The wealthy sinner he contemns,
Loves all that fear the Lord,
And tho' to his own hurt he swears,
Still he performs his word.　　　　　　　16

5. His hands disdain a golden bribe,
And never gripe the poor :
This man shall dwell with God on earth
And find his heav'n secure.　　　　　　　20

Volume I.　　　　　　　　　　H

PSALM XV. Long Metre.

Religion and justice, goodness and truth, or, Duties to God and man, or, The qualifications of a Christian.

Who shall ascend thy heav'nly place
Great God! and dwell before thy face?
The man that minds religion now,
And humbly walks with God below;　　　**4**

　2. Whose hands are pure, whose heart is clean,
Whose lips still speak the thing they mean;
No slanders dwell upon his tongue;
He hates to do his neighbour wrong.　　　**8**

　[3. Scarce will he trust an ill report,
Nor vent it to his neighbour's hurt:
Sinners of state he can despise,
But saints are honour'd in his eyes.]　　　**12**

　[4. Firm to his word he ever stood,
And always makes his promise good,
Nor dares to change the thing he swears
Whatever pain or loss he bears.]　　　**16**

　[5. He never deals in bribing gold,
And mourns that justice should be sold:
While others gripe and grind the poor
Sweet Charity attends his door.]　　　**20**

　6. He loves his enemies, and prays
For those that curse him to his face;
And doth to all men still the same
That he would hope or wish from them.　　　**24**

7. Yet when his holiest works are done
His soul depends on grace alone :
This is the man thy face shall see,
And dwell for ever Lord with thee ‡.   28

PSALM XVI. The first part. Long Metre.

Confession of our poverty, and saints the best company, or,
Good works profit men not God.

PRESERVE me Lord in time of need;
For succour to thy throne I flee,
But have no merits there to plead;
My goodness cannot reach to thee.   4

2. Oft' have my heart and tongue confest
How empty and how poor I am :
My praise can never make thee blest,
Nor add new glories to thy name.   8

3. Yet Lord thy saints on earth may reap
Some profit by the good we do :
These are the company I keep,
These are the choicest friends I know.   12

‡ Since our blessed Saviour in The New Testament has so much
explained the duties of the law and published the gospel, I could
not pass over this Psalm of the characters of the Jewish saint
without inserting some brighter articles that must belong to
the Christian, such as alms and charity to the poor, love to enemies, blessing those that curse us, doing to others as we would
have them do to us, and hope of acceptance only through divine grace.—I thought it necessary also to leave out the mention of usury, ver. 5. which though politically forbidden by
the Jews among themselves was never unlawful to the Gentiles, nor to any Christians since the Jewish polity expired.

H ij

4. Let others chufe the fons of mirth
To give a relifh to their wine,
I love the men of heav'nly birth,
Whofe thoughts and language are divine.   16

PSALM XVI. The fecond part. Long Metre.

Chrift's allfufficiency.

How faft their guilt and forrows rife
Who hafte to feek fome idol god!
I will not tafte their facrifice,
Their off'rings of forbidden blood.   4

2. My God provides a richer cup
And nobler food to live upon;
He for my life has offer'd up
Jefus, his beft-beloved Son.   8

3. His love is my perpetual feaft;
By day his counfels guide me right;
And be his name for ever bleft
Who gives me fweet advice by night.   12

4. I fet him ftill before mine eyes;
At my right hand he ftands prepar'd
To keep my foul from all furprife
And be my everlafting guard‡.   16

‡ From the Pfalmift's mention of drink-offerings of blood I
take occafion to allude to the facrifice of Chrift; *His flefh is
meat indeed, and his blood is drink indeed,* John vi. 55.

PSALM XVI. The third part. Long Metre.

Courage in death, and hope of the resurrection.

WHEN God is nigh my faith is strong,
His arm is my almighty prop :
Be glad my heart, rejoice my tongue,
My dying flesh shall rest in hope. 4

2. Tho' in the dust I lay my head,
Yet gracious God thou wilt not leave
My soul for ever with the dead,
Nor lose thy children in the grave. 8

3. My flesh shall thy first call obey,
Shake off the dust and rise on high;
Then shalt thou lead the wondrous way
Up to thy throne above the sky. 12

4. There streams of endless pleasure flow,
And full discov'ries of thy grace
(Which we but tasted here below)
Spread heav'nly joys thro' all the place †. 16

PSALM XVI. ver. 1,—8. The first part. Com. Metre.

Support and counsel from God without merit.

SAVE me O Lord from ev'ry foe ;
In thee my trust I place,
Tho' all the good that I can do
Can ne'er deserve thy grace. 4

† The last verses of this Psalm are applied only to Christ, *Acts* xiii. 36. and ii. 23. &c.; yet since they contain so fair a view of a resurrection, which is so seldom found in this book, I have formed these four stanzas into such expressions as may be assumed by Christians and applied to themselves.

H iij

2. Yet if my God prolong my breath
The faints may profit by 't,
The faints, the glory of the earth,
The men of my delight.   8

3. Let Heathens to their idols hafte
And worfhip wood or ftone,
But my delightful lot is caft
Where the true God is known.   1 2

4. His hand provides my conftant food,
He fills my daily cup ;
Much am I pleas'd with prefent good,
But more rejoice in hope.   16

5. God is my portion and my joy,
His counfels are my light,
He gives me fweet advice by day
And gentle hints by night   20

6. My foul would all her thoughts approve
To his allfeeing eye ;
Not death nor hell my hope fhall move
While fuch a friend is nigh.   24

PSALM XVI. The fecond part. Common Metre.

The death and refurrection of Chrift.

" I Set the Lord before my face,
" He bears my courage up ;
" My heart my tongue their joys exprefs,
" My flefh fhall reft in hope.   4

2. " My spirit Lord thou wilt not leave
" Where fouls departed are,
" Nor quit my body to the grave
" To fee corruption there.　　　　　　　8

3. " Thou wilt reveal the path of life
" And raife me to thy throne ;
" Thy courts immortal pleafure give,
" Thy prefence joys unknown."　　　　　12

[4. Thus in the name of Chrift the Lord
The holy David fung,
And Providence fulfils the word
Of his prophetick tongue.　　　　　　　16

5. Jefus. whom ev'ry faint adores,
Was crucify'd and flain;
Behold the tomb its prey reftores,
Behold he lives again !　　　　　　　　20

6. When fhall my feet arife and ftand
On heav'n's eternal hills?
There fits the Son at God's right hand,
And there the Father fmiles †]　　　　24

† In this verfion I have applied the three laft verfes of this
Pfalm to Chrift alone, as St. Peter applies them *Acts* ii. 23.;
yet inftead of the fourth line of the fecond ftanza, *To fee corruption there*, you may read thus, *To dwell for ever there*, and
then the three firft ftanzas may be fung alone, and applied to
every Chriftian.——Stanza ii. It is now agreed by the learned
that שָׁאוֹל *Sheol*, which is rendered *hell*, fignifies only the
ftate of the dead, that is, the grave for the body, and the fe-
parate ftate for the fpirit.

PSALM XVII. ver. 13. &c. Short Metre.

Portion of saints and sinners, or, *Hope and despair in death.*

ARISE my gracious God
And make the wicked flee;
They are but thy chastising rod
To drive thy saints to thee.   4

  2. Behold the sinner dies,
His haughty words are vain;
Here in this life his pleasure lies,
And all beyond is pain.   8

  3. Then let his pride advance,
And boast of all his store;
The Lord is my inheritance;
My soul can wish no more.   12

  4. I shall behold the face
Of my forgiving God,
And stand complete in righteousness
Wash'd in my Saviour's blood.   16

  5. There 's a new heav'n begun
When I awake from death,
Dress'd in the likeness of thy Son,
And draw immortal breath ‡.   20

‡ Stanza v. The heaven which souls enjoy in the separate state
is so much increased by the resurrection of the body that it
may be called a *new heaven,* the heaven of the body as well
as of the soul.

PSALM XVII. Long Metre.

*The sinner's portion and saint's hope, or, The heaven of
separate souls, and the resurrection.*

LORD I am thine; but thou wilt prove
My faith, my patience, and my love;
When men of spite against me join,
They are the sword, the hand is thine.　　　　4

2. Their hope and portion lies below;
'Tis all the happiness they know,
'Tis all they seek; they take their shares,
And leave the rest among their heirs.　　　　8

3. What sinners value I resign;
Lord 't is enough that thou art mine:
I shall behold thy blissful face,
And stand complete in righteousness.　　　　12

4. This life 's a dream, an empty show;
But the bright world to which I go
Hath joys substantial and sincere:
When shall I wake and find me there?　　　　16

5. O glorious hour! O bless'd abode!
I shall be near and like my God!
And flesh and sin no more control
The sacred pleasures of the soul.　　　　20

6. My flesh shall slumber in the ground
Till the last trumpet's joyful sound,
Then burst the chains with sweet surprise,
And in my Saviour's image rise ‡.   24

PSALM XVIII. ver. 1,—6, 15,—18. The first part.
Long Metre.

Deliverance from despair, or, *Temptations overcome.*

THEE will I love O Lord! my strength,
My rock, my tow'r, my high defence;
Thy mighty arm shall be my trust,
For I have found salvation thence.   4

2. Death and the terrours of the grave
Stood round me with their dismal shade,
While floods of high temptations rose
And made my sinking soul afraid.   8

‡ The sense of a great part of this Psalm occurs so often in
the book of Psalms that I thought it necessary to translate no
more than these few verses of it, namely, ver. 3. *Thou hast proved my heart, thou hast tried me, and shalt find nothing ;* ver.
13. *The wicked are thy sword ;* ver. 14. *The men of the world
have their portion in this life, whose belly thou fillest ; they leave
the rest of their substance to their babes ;* ver. 15. *I shall behold
thy face in righteousness, I shall be satisfied when I awake with
thy likeness.*—I confess I have indulged a large exposition here,
but I could not forbear to give my thoughts a loose upon this
divine description of complete blessedness in the 15th verse,
this bright abridgment of heaven.—From the word *awake* I
have taken occasion to represent the departing soul's *awaking*
into the world of spirits as well as the body's *awaking* from
the grave.

3. I faw the op'ning gates of hell,
With endlefs pains and forrows there
Which none but they that feel can tell,
While I was hurry'd to defpair.   12

4. In my diftrefs I call'd my God,
When I could fcarce believe him mine;
He bow'd his ear to my complaint,
Then did his grace appear divine.   16

.   [5. With fpeed he flew to my relief,
As on a cherub's wing he rode;
Awful and bright as lightning fhone
The face of my deliv'rer God.   20

6. Temptations fled at his rebuke,
The blaft of his almighty breath;
He fent falvation from on high,
And drew me from the depths of death.]   24

7. Great were my fears, my foes were great,
Much was their ftrength and more their rage;
But Chrift my Lord is conq'ror ftill
In all the wars that devils wage.   28

8. My fong for ever fhall record
That terrible that joyful hour,
And give the glory to the Lord,
Due to his mercy and his pow'r †.   32

† I have divided this long Pfalm into three parts, and accommodated the feveral verfes of it to our fpiritual warfare and victory through grace, as being of more frequent and general ufe to Chriftians; yet there are fo noble expreffions of triumph in God and thanks for victory over temporal enemies fcattered up and down, that perfuaded me to form them afterwards in common metre alfo, agreeable to their original defign.

PSALM XVIII. ver. 20,—26. The second part.
Long Metre.

Sincerity proved and rewarded.

LORD thou haft feen my foul fincere,
Haft made thy truth and love appear;
Before mine eyes I fet thy laws,
And thou haft own'd my righteous caufe.   4

   2. Since I have learn'd thy holy ways
I 'ave walk'd upright before thy face,
Or if my feet did e'er depart
'Twas never with a wicked heart.   8

   3. What fore temptations broke my reft!
What wars and ftrugglings in my breaft!
But thro' thy grace that reigns within
I guard againft my darling fin.   12

   4. That fin that clofe befets me ftill,
That works and ftrives againft my will,
When fhall thy Spirit's fov'reign pow'r
Deftroy it that it rife no more.   16

   [5. With an impartial hand the Lord
Deals out to mortals their reward:
The kind and faithful fouls fhall find
A God as faithful and as kind.   20

   6. The juft and pure fhall ever fay
Thou art more pure more juft than they;
And men that love revenge fhall know
God hath an arm of vengeance too.]   24

PSALM XVIII. ver. 30, 31, 34, 35, 46, &c.
The third part. Long Metre.

Rejoicing in God, or, Salvation and triumph.

Just are thy ways and true thy word,
Great Rock of my secure abode :
Who is a God beside the Lord,
Or where 's a refuge like our God? 4

2. 'Tis he that girds me with his might,
Gives me his holy sword to wield,
And while with sin and hell I fight
Spreads his salvation for my shield. 8

3. He lives, (and blessed be my Rock)
The God of my salvation lives!
The dark designs of hell are broke;
Sweet is the peace my Father gives. 12

4. Before the scoffers of the age
I will exalt my Father's name,
Nor tremble at their mighty rage,
But meet reproach and bear the shame. 16

5. To David and his royal seed
Thy grace for ever shall extend:
Thy love to saints in Christ their head
Knows not a limit nor an end. 20

PSALM XVIII. The first part. Common Metre.

Victory and triumph over temporal enemies.

We love thee Lord, and we adore;
Now is thine arm reveal'd;
Thou art our strength, our heav'nly tow'r,
Our bulwark and our shield. 4

2. We fly to our eternal Rock
And find a sure defence;
His holy name our lips invoke
And draw salvation thence. 8

3. When God our leader shines in arms
What mortal heart can bear
The thunder of his loud alarms,
The lightning of his spear? 12

4 He rides upon the winged wind,
And angels in array
In millions wait to know his mind,
And swift as flames obey. 16

5. He speaks, and at his fierce rebuke
Whole armies are dismay'd;
His voice, his frown, his angry look,
Strikes all their courage dead. 20

6. He forms our gen'rals for the field
With all their dreadful skill,
Gives them his awful sword to wield,
And makes their hearts of steel, 24

[7. He arms our captains to the fight;
(Tho' there his name 's forgot,
He girded Cyrus with his might,
But Cyrus knew him not.)   28
    8. Oft' has the Lord whole nations blest
For his own church's fake:
The pow'rs that give his people rest
Shall of his care partake †.]   32

PSALM XVIII. The second part. Common Metre.

The conqueror's song.

To thine almighty arm we owe
The triumphs of the day;
Thy terrours Lord confound the foe
And melt their strength away.   4
    2. 'Tis by thine aid our troops prevail
And break united pow'rs,
Or burn their boasted fleets, or scale
The proudest of their tow'rs.   8
    3. How have we chas'd them thro' the field
And trod them to the ground,
While thy salvation was our shield,
But they no shelter found!   12

† Stanza vii. Isa. xlv. 1, 5. *Thus saith the Lord to Cyrus——
I girded thee though thou hast not known me.*

I ij

4. In vain to idol saints they cry
And perish in their blood:
Where is a rock so great, so high,
So pow'rful, as our God?   16

5. The rock of Israel ever lives,
His name be ever blest;
'Tis his own arm the vict'ry gives,
And gives his people rest.   20

6. On kings that reign as David did
He pours his blessings down,
Secures their honours to their seed,
And well supports their crown.   24

PSALM XIX. The first part. Short Metre.

The book of Nature and Scripture.

For a Lord's day morning.

BEHOLD the lofty sky
Declares its maker God,
And all his starry works on high
Proclaim his pow'r abroad.   4

2. The darkness and the light
Still keep their course the same,
While night to day and day to night
Divinely teach his name.   8

3. In ev'ry diff'rent land
Their gen'ral voice is known;
They shew the wonders of his hand
And orders of his throne.   12

4. Ye Britith lands rejoice!
He here reveals his word :
We are not left to Nature's voice
To bid us know the Lord.   16

5. His statutes and commands
Are set before our eyes;
He puts his gospel in our hands,
Where our salvation lies.   20

6. His laws are just and pure;
His truth without deceit,
His promises for ever sure,
And his rewards are great.   24

7. [Not honey to the taste
Affords so much delight,
Nor gold that has the furnace past
So much allures the sight.   28

8. While of thy works I sing
Thy glory to proclaim,
Accept the praise my God, my King,
In my Redeemer's name *.]   32

* The Psalmist here and in other Psalms uses the word *law* to express the five books of Moses, or all the divine revelation that he had in his time; yet Christ and the Apostles so frequently distinguish the law and the gospel, that I have chosen to imitate their language, and have often introduced the words *gospel, truth*, and *promise*, instead of *statutes, testimonies, &c.* as being more agreeable to the style of The New Testament.—Stanza viii. I have here inserted the last verse of the Psalm with an evangelical turn, as a proper conclusion of this first part, the whole being too long to be sung at once according to our present custom.

I iij

PSALM XIX. The second part. Short Metre.

God's word most excellent, or, Sincerity and watchfulness.

For a Lord's day morning.

BEHOLD the morning sun
Begins his glorious way,
His beams thro' all the nations run
And life and light convey.   4

   2. But where the gospel comes
It spreads diviner light,
It calls dead sinners from their **tombs,**
And gives the blind their sight.   8

   3. How perfect is thy word!
And all thy judgments just;
For ever sure thy promise Lord,
And men securely trust.   12

   4. My gracious God how plain
Are thy directions giv'n!
O may I never read in vain,
But find the path to heav'n!   16

        PAUSE.
   5. I hear thy word with love,
And I would fain obey;
Send thy good Spirit from above
To guide me lest I stray.   20

6. O who can ever find
The errours of his ways?
Yet with a bold presumptuous mind
I would not dare transgress. 24

7. Warn me of ev'ry sin,
Forgive my secret faults,
And cleanse this guilty soul of mine,
Whose crimes exceed my thoughts. 28

8. While with my heart and tongue
I spread thy praise abroad,
Accept the worship and the song
My Saviour and my God. 32

PSALM XIX. Long Metre.

*The books of Nature and of Scripture compared, or, The
glory and success of the gospel.*

THE heav'ns declare thy glory Lord,
In ev'ry star thy wisdom shines,
But when our eyes behold thy word
We read thy name in fairer lines. 4

2. The rolling sun, the changing light,
And nights and days, thy pow'r confess,
But the best volume thou hast writ
Reveals thy justice and thy grace. 8

3. Sun, moon, and stars, convey thy praise
Round the whole earth, and never stand;
So when thy truth begun its race
It touch'd and glanc'd on ev'ry land. 12

5

4. Nor shall thy spreading gospel rest
Till thro' the world thy truth has run,
'Till Christ has all the nations blest
That see the light or feel the sun.   16

5. Great Sun of Righteousnefs arise,
Blefs the dark world with heav'nly light;
Thy gospel makes the simple wise,
Thy laws are pure, thy judgments right.   20

6. Thy noblest wonders here we view
In souls renew'd and sins forgiv'n:
Lord cleanse my sins, my soul renew,
And make thy word my guide to heav'n †.   24

PSALM XIX. To the tune of the 113th Psalm.

The book of Nature and Scripture.

GREAT God! the heav'n's wellorder'd frame
Declares the glories of thy name;
There thy rich works of wonder shine;
A thousand starry beauties there,
A thousand radiant marks, appear
Of boundless pow'r and skill divine.   6

---

† Though the plain design of the Psalmist is to shew the excellency of the book of Scripture above the book of Nature, in order to convert and save a sinner, yet the Apostle Paul, in *Rom.* x. 18. applies or accommodates the 4th verse to the spreading of the gospel over the Roman empire, which is called the *whole world* in The New Testament, and in this version I have endeavoured to imitate him.

2. From night to day from day to night,
The dawning and the dying light,
Lectures of heav'nly wisdom read;
With silent eloquence they raise
Our thoughts to our Creator's praise,
And neither sound nor language need. 12

3. Yet their divine instructions run
Far as the journies of the sun,
And ev'ry nation knows their voice.
The sun, like some young bridegroom dreſt,
Breaks from the chambers of the eaſt,
Rolls round, and makes the earth rejoice. 18

4. Where'er he ſpreads his beams abroad
He ſmiles, and ſpeaks his maker God;
All Nature joins to ſhew thy praiſe:
Thus God in ev'ry creature ſhines
Fair as the book of nature's lines,
But fairer is thy book of grace. 24

PAUSE.

5. I love the volumes of thy word;
What light and joy thoſe leaves afford
To ſouls benighted and diſtreſt!
Thy precepts guide my doubtful way,
Thy fear forbids my feet to ſtray,
Thy promiſe leads my heart to reſt. 30

6. From the diſcov'ries of thy law
The perfect rules of life I draw;

These are my study and delight :
Not honey so invites the taste,
Nor gold that hath the furnace past
Appears so pleasing to the sight.   36

7. Thy threat'nings wake my slumb'ring eyes
And warn me where my danger lies;
But 't is thy blessed gospel Lord
That makes my guilty conscience clean,
Converts my soul, subdues my sin,
And gives a free but large reward.   42

8. Who knows the errours of his thoughts?
My God forgive my secret faults,
And from presumptuous sins restrain :
Accept my poor attempts of praise
That I have read thy book of grace
And book of nature not in vain.   48

PSALM XX.

Prayer and hope of victory.

For a day of prayer in time of war.

Now may the God of pow'r and grace
Attend his people's humble cry!
Jehovah hears when Israel prays,
And brings deliv'rance from on high.   4

2. The name of Jacob's God defends
Better than shields or brazen walls;
He from his sanctuary sends
Succour and strength when Zion calls.   8

3 Well he remembers all our fighs,
His love exceeds our beft deferts;
His love accepts the facrifice
Of humble groans and broken hearts.   12

4. In his falvation is our hope,
And in the name of Ifrael's God   4
Our troops fhall lift their banners up,
Our navies fpread their flags abroad.   16

5. Some truft in horfes train'd for war,
And fome of chariots make their boafts;
Our fureft expectations are
From thee the Lord of heav'nly hofts.   20

[6. O may the mem'ry of thy name
Infpire our armies for the fight!
Our foes fhall fall and die with fhame,
Or quit the field with fhameful flight.]   24

7. Now fave us Lord! from flavifh fear,
Now let our hopes be firm and ftrong,
Till thy falvation fhall appear,
And joy and triumph raife the fong.   28

PSALM XXI. Common Metre.

Our king is the care of Heaven.

THE king O Lord! with fongs of praife
Shall in thy ftrength rejoice,
And blefs'd with thy falvation raife
To heav'n his cheerful voice.   4

2. Thy sure defence thro' nations round
Has spread his glorious name,
And his successful actions crown'd
With majesty and fame.   8

3. Then let the king on God alone
For timely aid rely;
His mercy shall support the throne,
And all our wants supply.   12

4. But righteous Lord! his stubborn foes
Shall feel thy dreadful hand;
Thy vengeful arm shall find out those
That hate his mild command.   16

5. When thou against them dost engage,
Thy just but dreadful doom
Shall like a fiery oven's rage
Their hopes and them consume.   20

6. Thus Lord! thy wondrous pow'r declare,
And thus exalt thy fame,
Whilst we glad songs of praise prepare
For thine almighty name *.   24

PSALM XXI. ver. 1,—9. Long Metre.

Christ exalted to the kingdom.

David rejoic'd in God his strength,
Rais'd to the throne by special grace,
But Christ the Son appears at length,
Fulfils the triumph and the praise.   4

* I have borrowed almost all these stanzas from Mr. Tate's
version, and they seem very applicable to his present Majesty
King George, 1716.

2. How great is the Meſſiah's joy
In the ſalvation of thy hand!
Lord thou haſt rais'd his kingdom high,
And giv'n the world to his command. 8

3. Thy goodneſs grants whate'er he will,
Nor doth the leaſt requeſt withhold,
Bleſſings of love prevent him ſtill,
And crowns of glory not of gold. 12

4. Honour and majeſty divine
Around his ſacred temples ſhine ;
Bleſs'd with the favour of thy face,
And length of everlaſting days. 16

5. Thine hand ſhall find out all his foes;
And as a fiery oven glows
With raging heat and living coals,
So ſhall thy wrath devour their ſouls. 20

PSALM XXII. ver. 1,——16. The firſt part.
Common Metre.

The ſufferings and death of Chriſt.

Why has my God my ſoul forſook,
Nor will a ſmile afford ?
(Thus David once in anguiſh ſpoke,
And thus our dying Lord.) 4

2. Tho' it is thy chief delight to dwell
Among thy praifing faints,
Yet thou canft hear a groan as well,
And pity our complaints.   8

3. Our fathers trufted in thy name
And great deliv'rance found,
But I 'm a worm defpis'd of men,
And trodden to the ground.   12

4. Shaking the head they pafs me by
And laugh my foul to fcorn;
" In vain he trufts in God," they cry,
" Neglected and forlorn."   16

5. But thou art he who form'd my flefh
By thine almighty word,
And fince I hung upon the breaft
My hope is in the Lord.   20

6. Why will my Father hide his face
When foes ftand threat'ning round,
In the dark hour of deep diftrefs,
And not an helper found?   24

PAUSE.

7. Behold thy darling left among
The cruel and the proud,
As bulls of Bafhan fierce and ftrong,
As lions roaring loud.   28

8. From earth and hell my forrows meet
To multiply the fmart;
They nail my hands, they pierce my feet,
And try to vex my heart.   32

9. Yet if thy sov'reign hand let loose
The rage of earth and hell,
Why will my heav'nly Father bruise
The Son he loves so well ?   36

10. My God, if possible it be,
Withhold this bitter cup;
But I resign my will to thee,
And drink the sorrows up.   40

11. My heart dissolves with pangs unknown,
In groans I waste my breath :
Thy heavy hand has brought me down
Low as the dust of death.   ·   44

12. Father, I give my spirit up,
And trust it in thy hand ;
My dying flesh shall rest in hope,
And rise at thy command.   48

PSALM XXII. ver. 20, 21, 27,——31. The second part.
Common Metre.

Christ's sufferings and kingdom.

" Now from the roaring lion's rage
" O Lord! protect thy Son,
" Nor leave thy darling to engage
" The pow'rs of hell alone."   4

K ij

2. Thus did our fuff'ring Saviour pray
With mighty cries and tears;
God heard him in that dreadful day
And chas'd away his fears.   8

3. Great was the vict'ry of his death,
His throne exalted high,
And all the kindreds of the earth
Shall worfhip or fhall die.   12

4. A num'rous offspring mnft arife
From his expiring groans,
They fhall be reckon'd in his eyes
For daughters and for fons.   16

5. The meek and humble fouls fhall fee
His table richly fpread,
And all that feek the Lord fhall be
With joys immortal fed.   20

6. The ifles fhall know the righteoufnefs
Of our incarnate God,
And nations yet unborn profefs
Salvation in his blood.   24

PSALM XXII. Long Metre.

Chrift's fufferings and exaltation.

Now let our mournful fongs record
The dying forrows of our Lord,
When he complain'd in tears and blood
As one forfaken of his God.

2. The Jews beheld him thus forlorn,
And shake their heads and laugh in scorn:
" He rescu'd others from the grave,
" Now let him try himself to save.   8

   3. " This is the man did once pretend
" God was his father and his friend:
" If God the blessed lov'd him so
" Why doth he fail to help him now?"   12

   4. Barbarous people! cruel priests!
How they stood round like savage beasts,
Like lions gaping to devour,
When God had left him in their pow'r.   16

   5. They wound his head, his hands, his feet,
Till streams of blood each other meet,
By lot his garments they divide,
And mock the pangs in which he dy'd.   20

   6. But God his Father heard his cry;
Rais'd from the dead he reigns on high:
The nations learn his righteousness,
And humble sinners taste his grace †.   24

† In this version I have abridged the whole Psalm, and chosen only those verses of it which are cited or explained in The
New Testament, namely, 1, 7, 8, 12, 13, 16, 18, 24, 28, 29, 31.

PSALM XXIII. Long Metre.

God our Shepherd.

My Shepherd is the living Lord;
Now shall my wants be well supply'd;
His providence and holy word
Become my safety and my guide.   4

2. In pastures where salvation grows
He makes me feed, he makes me rest,
There living water gently flows,
And all the food divinely blest.   8

3. My wand'ring feet his ways mistake,
But he restores my soul to peace,
And leads me for his mercy's sake
In the fair paths of righteousness.   12

4. Tho' I walk thro' the gloomy vale
Where death and all its terrours are,
My heart and hope shall never fail,
For God my Shepherd 's with me there.   16

5. Amidst the darkness and the deeps
Thou art my comfort, thou my stay,
Thy staff supports my feeble steps,
Thy rod directs my doubtful way.   20

6. The sons of earth and sons of hell
Gaze at thy goodness, and repine
To see my table spread so well
With living bread and cheerful wine.   24

[7. How I rejoice when on my head
Thy Spirit condefcends to reft!
'Tis a divine anointing, fhed
Like oil of gladnefs at a feaft. 28

8. Surely the mercies of the Lord
Attend his houfehold all their days;
There will I dwell to hear his word,
To feek his face and fing his praife.] 32

PSALM XXIII. Common Metre.

My Shepherd will fupply my need,
Jehovah is his name,
In paftures frefh he makes me feed
Befide the living ftream. 4

2. He brings my wand'ring fpirit back
When I forfake his ways,
And leads me for his mercy's fake
In paths of truth and grace. 8

3. When I walk thro' the fhades of death
Thy prefence is my ftay;
A word of thy fupporting breath
Drives all my fears away. 12

4. Thy hand in fpite of all my foes
Doth ftill my table fpread,
My cup with bleffings overflows,
Thine oil anoints my head. 16

5. The fure provifions of my God
Attend me all my days;
O may thy houfe be mine abode,
And all my work be praife!   20

6. There would I find a fettled reft
While others go and come,
No more a ftranger or a gueft,
But like a child at home *.   24

PSALM XXIII. Short Metre.

THE Lord my Shepherd is,
I fhall be well fupply'd ;
Since he is mine and I am his
What can I want befide ?   4

2. He leads me to the place
Where heav'nly pafture grows,
Where living waters gently pafs,
And full falvation flows..   8

3. If e'er I go aftray
He doth my foul reclaim,
And guides me in his own right way
For his moft holy name.   12

* Stanza iv. The oil or ointment that was ufed of old to
anoint and perfume the head; in the fenfe and language of
The New Teftament muft fignify the communications of the
Holy Spirit, which is called *the anointing*, 1 John ii. 20, 27. as
I have explained it in the long metre, and *Pfal.* xlv. 47. with
John lii. 34. approves it.

4. While he affords his aid
I cannot yield to fear
Tho' I fhould walk thro' death's dark fhade;
My Shepherd 's with me there.   16

  5. In fpite of all my foes
Thou doft my table fpread,
My cup with bleffings overflows,
And joy exalts my head.   20

  6. The bounties of thy love
Shall crown my following days,
Nor from thy houfe will I remove,
Nor ceafe to fpeak thy praife.   24

PSALM XXIV. Common Metre.

Dwelling with God.

THE earth for ever is the Lord's
With Adam's num'rous race,
He rais'd its arches o'er the floods,
And built it on the feas.   4

  2. But who among the fons of men
May vifit thine abode?
He that has hands from mifchief clean,
Whofe heart is right with God.   8

  3. This is the man may rife and take
The bleffings of his grace,
This is the lot of thofe that feek
The God of Jacob's face.   12

4. Now let our fouls' immortal pow'rs
To meet the Lord prepare,
Lift up their everlafting doors,
The King of glory 's near.   16

5. The King of glory! who can tell
The wonders of his might?
He rules the nations, but to dwell
With faints is his delight.   20

PSALM XXIV. Long Metre.

Saints dwell in heaven, or, Chrift's afcenfion.

This fpacious earth is all the Lord's,
And men and worms, and beafts and birds,
He rais'd the buildings on the feas,
And gave it for their dwelling-place.   4

2. But there 's a brighter world on high,
Thy palace Lord above the fky:
Who fhall afcend that bleft abode,
And dwell fo near his maker God?   8

3. He that abhors and fears to fin,
Whofe heart is pure, whofe hands are clean,
Him fhall the Lord the Saviour blefs,
And clothe his foul with righteoufnefs.   12

4. Thefe are the men, the pious race,
That feek the God of Jacob's face,
Thefe fhall enjoy the blifsful fight,
And dwell in everlafting light.   16

PAUSE.

5. Rejoice ye shining worlds on high,
Behold the King of glory nigh!
Who can this King of glory be?
The mighty Lord the Saviour 's he. 20

6. Ye heav'nly gates your leaves display
To make the Lord the Saviour way;
Laden with spoils from earth and hell
The Conq'ror comes with God to dwell. 24

7. Rais'd from the dead he goes before,
He opens heav'n's eternal door,
To give his saints a blest abode
Near their Redeemer and their God †. 28

PSALM XXV. ver. 1,—11. The first part.

Waiting for pardon and direction.

I Lift my Soul to God,
My trust is in his name,
Let not my foes that seek my blood
Still triumph in my shame. 4

† If this Psalm was written at the ascent of the ark of God
into Zion, the city of David, it is not unnatural to apply it to
the presence of Christ with his church in worship, as in the
common metre, or to the ascension of Christ to heaven, as in
this metre. In this and other parts of the Psalm I have endeavoured to make the connexion plain and easy, which is very
obscure in the text.

2. Sin and the pow'rs of hell
Perfuade me to defpair;
Lord make me know thy cov'nant well
'That I may 'fcape the fnare.   8

3. From the firft dawning light
Till the dark ev'ning rife
For thy falvation Lord I wait
With ever-longing eyes.   12

4. Remember all thy grace,
And lead me in thy truth,
Forgive the fins of riper days
And follies of my youth.   16

5. The Lord is juft and kind,
The meek fhall learn his ways,
And ev'ry humble finner find
The methods of his grace.   20

6. For his own goodnefs' fake
He faves my foul from fhame;
He pardons (tho' my guilt be great)
Thro' my Redeemer's name.   24

PSALM XXV. ver. 12, 14, 10, 13. Second part.

Divine inftruction.

WHERE fhall the man be found
That fears t' offend his God,
That loves the gofpel's joyful found,
And trembles at the rod?   4

    2

2. The Lord shall make him know
The secrets of his heart,
The wonders of his cov'nant show,
And all his love impart. 8

3. The dealings of his hand
Are truth and mercy still
With such as to his cov'nant stand
And love to do his will. 12

4. Their soul shall dwell at ease
Before their Maker's face,
Their seed shall taste the promises
In their extensive grace. 16

PSALM XXV. ver. 15,—22. The third part.

Distress of soul, or, *Backsliding and desertion.*

MINE eyes and my desire
Are ever to the Lord;
I love to plead his promises
And rest upon his word. 4

2. Turn turn thee to my soul,
Bring thy salvation near;
When will thy hand release my feet
Out of the deadly snare? 8

3. When shall the sov'reign grace
Of my forgiving God
Restore me from those dang'rous ways
My wand'ring feet have trod? 12

4. The tumult of my thoughts
Doth but enlarge my wo;
My fpirit languifhes, my heart
Is defolate and low.   16

5. With ev'ry morning light
My forrow new begins:
Look on my anguifh and my pain,
And pardon all my fins.   20

PAUSE.

6. Behold the hofts of hell,
How cruel is their hate?
Againft my life they rife and join
Their fury with deceit.   24

7. O keep my foul from death,
Nor put my hope to fhame,
For I have plac'd my only truft
In my Redeemer's name.   28

8. With humble faith I wait
To fee thy face again;
Of Ifrael it ne'er fhall be faid
He fought the Lord in vain.   32

PSALM XXVI.

Self-examination, or, *Evidences of grace.*

Judge me O Lord and prove my ways,
And try my reins and try my heart;
My faith upon thy promife ftays,
Nor from thy law my feet depart.   4

2. I hate to walk I hate to sit
With men of vanity and lies:
The scoffer and the hypocrite
Are the abhorrence of mine eyes.   8

3. Amongst thy saints will I appear
With hands wellwash'd in innocence,
But when I stand before thy bar
The blood of Christ is my defence.   12

4. I love thy habitation Lord,
The temple where thine honours dwell,
There shall I hear thine holy word,
And there thy works of wonder tell.   16

5. Let not my soul be join'd at last
With men of treachery and blood,
Since I my days on earth have past
Among the saints and near my God.   20

PSALM XXVII. ver. 1,—6. The first part.

The church is our delight and safety.

THE Lord of glory is my light
And my salvation too;
God is my strength, nor will I fear
What all my foes can do. $\overline{4}$

2. One privilege my heart desires;
O grant me an abode
Among the churches of thy saints,
The temples of my God!   8

3. There shall I offer my requests,
And see thy beauty still,
Shall hear thy messages of love,
And there inquire thy will.

4. When troubles rise and storms appear
There may his children hide;
God has a strong pavilion where
He makes my soul abide.

5. Now shall my head be lifted high
Above my foes around,
And songs of joy and victory
Within thy temple found.

PSALM XXVII. ver. 8, 9, 13, 14. Second part.

Prayer and hope.

Soon as I heard my Father say
" Ye children seek my grace,"
My heart reply'd without delay,
" I 'll seek my Father's face."

2. Let not thy face be hid from me,
Nor frown my soul away;
God of my life I fly to thee
In a distressing day.

3. Should friends and kindred near and dear
Leave me to want or die
My God would make my life his care,
And all my need supply.

4. My fainting flesh had dy'd with grief
Had not my soul believ'd
To see thy grace provide relief,
Nor was my hope deceiv'd. 16

5. Wait on the Lord ye trembling saints
And keep your courage up,
He 'll raise your spirit when it faints,
And far exceed your hope *. 20

PSALM XXIX.

Storm and thunder.

Give to the Lord ye sons of Fame,
Give to the Lord renown and pow'r,
Ascribe due honours to his name,
And his eternal might adore. 4

2. The Lord proclaims his pow'r aloud
Over the ocean and the land,
His voice divides the wat'ry cloud,
And lightnings blaze at his command. 8

3. He speaks, and tempest, hail, and wind,
Lay the wide forests bare around;
The fearful hart and frighted hind
Leap at the terrour of the sound. 12

* The xxviiith Psalm has scarce any thing new but what is
repeated in other Psalms.

4. To Lebanon he turns his voice,
And lo! the stately cedars break,
The mountains tremble at the noise,
The vallies roar the deserts quake.   16

5. The Lord sits sov'reign on the flood,
The Thund'rer reigns for ever King,
But makes his church his blest abode,
Where we his awful glories sing.   20

6. In gentler language there the Lord
The counsels of his grace imparts:
Amidst the raging storm his word
Speaks peace and courage to our hearts.   24

PSALM XXX. The first part.

Sickness healed and sorrow removed.

I Will extol thee Lord on high,
At thy command diseases fly:
Who but a God can speak and save
From the dark borders of the grave?   4

2. Sing to the Lord ye saints of his,
And tell how large his goodness is;
Let all your pow'rs rejoice, and bless
While you record his holiness.   8

3. His anger but a moment stays;
His love is life and length of days:
'Tho' grief and tears the night employ
The morning-star restores the joy.   12

PSALM XXX. ver. 6. The second part.

Health, sickness, and recovery.

FIRM was my health, my day was bright,
And I presum'd 't would ne'er be night,
Fondly I said within my heart
" Pleasure and peace shall ne'er depart." 4

2. But I forgot thine arm was strong
Which made my mountain stand so long;
Soon as thy face began to hide
My health was gone my comforts dy'd. 8

3. I cry'd aloud to thee my God,
" What canst thou profit by my blood?
" Deep in the dust can I declare
" Thy truth, or sing thy goodness there? 12

4. " Hear me, O God of grace," I said,
" And bring me from among the dead:"
Thy word rebuk'd the pains I felt,
Thy pard'ning love remov'd my guilt. 16

5. My groans, and tears, and forms of wo,
Are turn'd to joy and praises now;
I throw my sackcloth on the ground,
And ease and gladness gird me round. 20

6. My tongue, the glory of my frame,
Shall ne'er be silent of thy name;
Thy praise shall sound thro' earth and heav'n
For sickness heal'd and sins forgiv'n. 24

PSALM XXXI. ver. 5, 13,—19, 22, 23. Firſt part.

Deliverance from death.

INTO thine hand O God of truth
My ſpirit I commit,
Thou haſt redeem'd my ſoul from death
And ſav'd me from the pit.   4

2. The paſſions of my hope and fear
Maintain'd a doubtful ſtrife
While ſorrow, pain, and ſin, conſpir'd
To take away my life.   8

3. " My times are in thine hand," I cry'd,
" Tho' I draw near the duſt :"
Thou art the refuge where I hide,
The God in whom I truſt.   12

4. O make thy reconciled face
Upon thy ſervant ſhine,
And ſave me for thy mercy's ſake,
For I 'm entirely thine.   16

PAUSE.

5. ['Twas in my haſte my ſpirit ſaid
" I muſt deſpair and die,
" I am cut off before thine eyes;"
But thou haſt heard my cry.]   20

6. Thy goodneſs how divinely free!
How wondrous is thy grace
To thoſe that fear thy majeſty
And truſt thy promiſes!   24

7 O love the Lord all ye his saints
And sing his praises loud,
He 'll bend his ear to your complaints
And recompense the proud. 28

PSALM XXXI. ver. 7,—13, 18,—21. Second part.

Deliverance from slander and reproach.

My heart rejoices in thy name
My God, my help, my trust;
Thou hast preserv'd my face from shame,
Mine honour from the dust. 4

2. " My life is spent with grief," I cry'd,
" My years consum'd in groans,
" My strength decays, mine eyes are dry'd,
" And sorrow wastes my bones." 8

3. Among mine enemies my name
Was a mere proverb grown,
While to my neighbours I became
Forgotten and unknown. 12

4. Slander and fear on ev'ry side
Seiz'd and beset me round,
I to the throne of grace apply'd
And speedy rescue found. 16

PAUSE.

5. How great deliv'rance thou hast wrought
Before the sons of men!
The lying lips to silence brought,
And made their boastings vain. 20

5. Thy children from the ftrife of tongues
Shall thy pavilion hide,
Guard them from infamy and wrongs,
And crufh the fons of pride.   24

7. Within thy fecret prefence Lord
Let me for ever dwell,
No fenced city wall'd and barr'd
Secures a faint fo well †.   28

PSALM XXXII. Short Metre.

Forgivenefs of fin upon confeffion.

O Bleffed fouls are they
Whofe fins are cover'd o'er!
Divinely blefs'd to whom the Lord
Imputes their guilt no more.   4

2. They mourn their follies paft,
And keep their hearts with care;
Their lips and lives without deceit
Shall prove their faith fincere.   8

3. While I conceal'd my guilt
I felt the feft'ring wound,
Till I confefs'd my fins to thee
And ready pardon found.   12

† I have much tranfpofed the parts of this Pfalm, that I
might unite the verfes of the fame fenfe and fubject nearer together, and contract them into two divine hymns.

4. Let finners learn.to pray,
Let faints keep near the throne :
Our help in times of deep diftrefs
Is found in God alone.　　　　　16

PSALM XXXII. Common Metre.

Free pardon and fincere obedience, or, *Confeffion and for-
giveneſs.*

HAPPY the man to whom his God
No more imputes his fin,
But wafh'd in the Redeemer's blood
Hath made his garments clean :　　4
　2. Happy beyond expreffion he
Whofe debts are thus difcharg'd,
And from the guilty bondage free
He feels his foul eniarg'd.　　　8
　3. His fpirit hates deceit and lies,
His words are all fincere ;
He guards his heart, he guards his eyes,
To keep his confcience clear.　　12
　4. While I my inward guilt fuppreft
No quiet could I find ;
Thy wrath lay burning in my breaft
And rack'd my tortur'd mind.　　16
　5. Then I confefs'd my troubled thoughts,
My fecret fins reveal'd ;
Thy pard'ning grace forgave my faults,
Thy grace my pardon feal'd.　　20

6. This shall invite thy saints to pray :
When like a raging flood
Temptations rise, our strength and stay
Is a forgiving God.   24

PSALM XXXII. First part. Long Metre.

*Repentanceandfreepardon,*or,*Justificationandsanctification.*

BLESS'D is the man, for ever bless'd,
Whose guilt is pardon'd by his God,
Whose sins with sorrow are confess'd,
And cover'd with his Saviour's blood.   4

2. Bless'd is the man to whom the Lord
Imputes not his iniquities;
He pleads no merit of reward,
And not on works but grace relies.   8

3. From guile his heart and lips are free ;
His humble joy his holy fear
With deep repentance well agree,
And join to prove his faith sincere.   12

4. How glorious is that righteousness
That hides and cancels all his sins!
While a bright evidence of grace
Thro' his whole life appears and shines *.   16

* These two first verses of this Psalm being cited by the apostle
In the ivth chapter of *Romans*, to shew the freedom of our
pardon and justification by grace without works, I have in this
version of it enlarged the sense by mention of the blood of
Christ and faith and repentance ; and because the Psalmist adds
—*a spirit in which is no guile*, I have inserted that sincere
obedience which is a scriptural evidence of our faith and
justification.

PSALM XXXII. Second part. Long Metre.

A guilty conscience eased by confession and pardon.

WHILE I keep silence and conceal
My heavy guilt within my heart,
What torments doth my conscience feel;
What agonies of inward smart!   4

  2. I spread my sins before the Lord,
And all my secret faults confess;
Thy gospel speaks a pard'ning word,
Thine holy Spirit seals the grace.   8

  3. For this shall ev'ry humble soul
Make swift addresses to thy seat;
When floods of huge temptations roll
There shall they find a bless'd retreat.   12

  4. How safe beneath thy wings I lie,
When days grow dark and storms appear!
And when I walk thy watchful eye
Shall guide me safe from ev'ry snare.   16

PSALM XXXIII. First part. Common Metre.

Works of creation and Providence.

REJOICE ye righteous in the Lord;
This work belongs to you:
Sing of his name, his ways, his word,
How holy, just and true.

2. His mercy and his righteousness
Let heav'n and earth proclaim,
His works of nature and of grace
Reveal his wondrous name.

3. His wisdom and almighty word
The heav'nly arches spread,
And by the Spirit of the Lord
Their shining hosts were made.

4. He bid the liquid waters flow
To their appointed deep;
The flowing seas their limits know,
And their own station keep.

5. Ye tenants of the spacious earth
With fear before him stand;
He spake, and nature took its birth,
And rests on his command.

6. He scorns the angry nations' rage,
And breaks their vain designs;
His counsel stands thro' ev'ry age,
And in full glory shines.

PSALM XXXIII. Second part. Common Metre.

Creatures vain and God allsufficient.

Bless'd is the nation where the Lord
Hath fix'd his gracious throne,
Where he reveals his heav'nly word,
And calls their tribes his own.

2. His eye with infinite furvey
Does the whole world behold;
He form'd us all of equal clay,
And knows our feeble mould. 8

3. Kings are not refcu'd by the force
Of armies from the grave,
Nor fpeed nor courage of an horfe
Can the bold rider fave. 12

4. Vain is the ftrength of beafts or men
To hope for fafety thence,
But holy fouls from God obtain
A ftrong and fure defence. 16

5. God is their fear and God their truft
When plagues or famine fpread;
His watchful eye fecures the juft
Among ten thoufand dead. 20

6 Lord let our hearts in thee rejoice,
And blefs us from thy throne,
For we have made thy word our choice,
And truft thy grace alone. 24

PSALM XXXIII. as the 113th Pfalm. Firft part.

Works of creation and Providence.

Ye holy fouls in God rejoice,
Your Maker's praife becomes your voice:
Great is your theme, your fongs be new;
Sing of his name, his word, his ways,
His works of nature and of grace,
How wife and holy, juft and true. 6

2. Juftice and truth he ever loves,
And the whole earth his goodnefs proves:
His word the heav'nly arches fpread,
How wide they fhine from north to fouth!
And by the Spirit of his mouth
Were all the ftarry armies made.   13

3. He gathers the wide flowing feas:
Thofe wat'ry treafures know their place
In the vaft ftorehoufe of the deep:
He fpake, and gave all nature birth,
And fires, and feas, and heav'n, and earth,
His everlafting orders keep.   18

4. Let mortals tremble and adore
A God of fuch refiftlefs pow'r,
Nor dare indulge their feeble rage:
Vain are your thoughts and weak your hands,
But his eternal counfel ftands,
And rules the world from age to age.   24

PSALM XXXIII. as the 113th Pfalm. Second part.

Creatures vain and God allfufficient.

O Happy nation where the Lord
Reveals the treafure of his word,
And builds his church, his earthly throne!
His eye the Heathen world furveys,
He form'd their hearts, he knows their ways,
But God their Maker is unknown.   6

2. Let kings rely upon their hoft,
And of his ftrength the champion boaft:
In vain they boaft, in vain rely;
In vain we truft the brutal force
Or fpeed or courage of a horfe
To guard his rider or to fly. 12

3. The eye of thy compaffion Lord
Doth more fecure defence afford
When deaths or dangers threat'ning ftand: ·
Thy watchful eye preferves the juft
Who make thy name their fear and truft
When wars or famine wafte the land. 18

4. In ficknefs or the bloody field
Thou our Phyfician, thou our Shield,
Send us falvation from thy throne:
We wait to fee thy goodnefs fhine,
Let us rejoice in help divine,
For all our hope is God alone. 24

PSALM XXXIV. Firft part. Long Metre.

God's care of the faints, or, *Deliverance by prayer*

LORD, I will blefs thee all my days,
Thy praife fhall dwell upon my tongue;
My foul fhall glory in thy grace,
While faints rejoice to hear the fong. 4

2. Come, magnify the Lord with me,
Come, let us all exalt his name;
I sought th' eternal God, and he
Has not expos'd my hope to shame.   8

3. I told him all my secret grief;
My secret groaning reach'd his ears,
He gave my inward pains relief,
And calm'd the tumult of my fears.   12

4. To him the poor lift up their eyes,
Their faces feel the heav'nly shine;
A beam of mercy from the skies
Fills them with light and joy divine.   16

5. His holy angels pitch their tents
Around the men that serve the Lord;
O fear and love him all his saints,
Taste of his grace and trust his word.   20

6. The wild young lions pinch'd with pain
And hunger roar thro' all the wood,
But none shall seek the Lord in vain,
Nor want supplies of real good.   24

PSALM XXXIV. ver. 11,—22. Second part.
Long Metre.

Religious education, or, Instructions of piety.

CHILDREN in years and knowledge young,
Your parents' hope your parents' joy,
Attend the counsels of my tongue;
Let pious thoughts your minds employ.   4

2. If you defire a length of days,
And peace to crown your mortal ftate,
Reftrain your feet from impious ways,
Your lips from flander and deceit. 8

3. The eyes of God regard his faints,
His ears are open to their cries;
He fets his frowning face againft
The fons of violence and lies. 12

4 To humble fouls and broken hearts
God with his grace is ever nigh;
Pardon and hope his love imparts
When men in deep contrition lie. 16

5. He tells their tears, he counts their groans,
His Son redeems their fouls from death;
His Spirit heals their broken bones,
They in his praife employ their breath. 20

PSALM XXXIV. ver. 1,——1c. Firft part.
Common Metre.

Prayer and praife for eminent deliverance.

I'LL blefs the Lord from day to day;
How good are all his ways!
Ye humble fouls that ufe to pray
Come help my lips to praife. 4

2. Sing to the honour of his name
How a poor fuff'rer cry'd,
Nor was his hope expos'd to fhame,
Nor was his fuit deny'd. 8

3. When threat'ning forrows round me ftood,
And endlefs fears arofe,
Like the loud billows of a flood
Redoubling all my woes,   12

4. I told the Lord my fore diftrefs
With heavy groans and tears,
He gave my fharpeft torments eafe,
And filenc'd all my fears.   16

PAUSE.

5. [O finners come and tafte his love,
Come learn his pleafant ways,
And let your own experience prove
The fweetnefs of his grace.   20

6. He bids his angels pitch their tents
Round where his children dwell;
What ills their heav'nly care prevents
No earthly tongue can tell.]   24

7. [O love the Lord ye faints of his;
His eye regards the juft;
How richly bleft their portion is
Who make the Lord their truft!   28

8. Young lions pinch'd with hunger roar
And famifh in the wood,
But God fupplies his holy poor
With ev'ry needful good.].   32

PSALM XXXIV. ver. 11,—22. Second part.
Common Metre.

Exhortations to peace and holiness.

COME children learn to fear the Lord;
And that your days be long
Let not a false or spiteful word
Be found upon your tongue. 4

2. Depart from mischief, practise love,
Pursue the works of peace,
So shall the Lord your ways approve
And set your souls at ease. 8

3. His eyes awake to guard the just,
His ears attend their cry :
When broken spirits dwell in dust
The God of grace is nigh. 12

4. What tho' the sorrows here they taste
Are sharp and tedious too?
The Lord who saves them all at last
Is their supporter now. 16

5. Evil shall smite the wicked dead,
But God secures his own,
Prevents the mischief when they slide,
Or heals the broken bone. 20

6. When desolation like a flood
O'er the proud sinner rolls,
Saints find a refuge in their God,
For he redeem'd their souls. 24

I

PSALM XXXV. ver. I,—9. Firſt part. Common Metre.

Prayer and faith of perſecuted ſaints, or, Imprecations mixed with charity.

Now plead my cauſe almighty God
With all the ſons of ſtrife,
And fight againſt the men of blood
Who fight againſt my life.   4

   2. Draw out thy ſpear and ſtop their way,
Lift thine avenging rod,
But to my ſoul in mercy ſay
" I am thy Saviour God."   8

   3. They plant their ſnares to catch my feet,
And nets of miſchief ſpread;
Plunge the deſtroyers in the pit
That their own hands have made.   12

   4. Let fogs and darkneſs hide their way,
And ſlipp'ry be their ground;
Thy wrath ſhall make their lives a prey,
And all their rage confound.   16

   5. They fly like chaff before the wind,
Before thine angry breath;
The angel of the Lord behind
Purſues them down to death.   20

   6. They love the road that leads to hell;
Then let the rebels die
Whoſe malice is implacable
Againſt the Lord on high.   24

7. But if thou haft a chofen few
Amongft that impious race,
Divide them from the bloody crew
By thy furprifing grace. 28

8. Then will I raife my tuneful voice
To make thy wonders known;
In their falvation I 'll rejoice,
And blefs thee for my own †. 32

PSALM XXXV. ver. 12, 13, 14. Second part.

Love to enemies, or, *The love of Chrift to finners typified in David.*

BEHOLD the love, the gen'rous love,
That holy David fhows;
Hark how his founding bowels move
To his afflicted foes! 4

† Stanza vi. Among the imprecations that David ufes againft his adverfaries in this Pfalm I have adventured to turn the edge of fome of them away from perfonal enemies againit the implacable enemies of God in the world.---Stanza vii, viii. Agreeably to the fpirit of the gofpel I have here further mollified thefe imprecations by a charitable diftinction and petition for their fouls, which fpirit of evangelick charity appears fo confpicuous in the 12th, 13th, and 14th verfes of the Pfalm, that I could not forbear to form them into a fhort diftinct hymn, enlarging on that glorious character of a Chriftian *love to our enemies,* commanded fo particularly, and fo divinely exemplified, by Chrift himfelf.

2. When they are fick his foul complains,
And feems to feel the fmart;
The fpirit of the gofpel reigns
And melts his pious heart.   8

3. How did his flowing tears condole
. As for a brother dead!
And fafting mortify'd his foul,
While for their life he pray'd.   12

4. They groan'd and curs'd him on their bed,
Yet ftill he pleads and mourns,
And double bleffings on his head
The righteous God returns.   16

5. O glorious type of heav'nly grace!
Thus Chrift the Lord appears;
While finners curfe the Saviour prays,
And pities them with tears.   20

6. He the true David, Ifrael's King,
Blefs'd and belov'd of God,
To fave us rebels dead in fin
Pay'd his own deareft blood *.   24

PSALM XXXVI. ver. 5,——9. Long Metre.

*The perfeftions and providence of God, or, General provi-
dence and fpecial grace.*

High in the heav'ns eternal God!
Thy goodnefs in full glory fhines;
Thy truth fhall break thro' ev'ry cloud
That veils and darkens thy defigns.   4

---

* See the Notes on the firft part of this Pfalm.----Stanza I.
Sounding of the bowels is a fcriptural metaphor, *Ifa.* lxiii. 15.

2. For ever firm thy juſtice ſtands
As mountains their foundations keep;
Wiſe are the wonders of thy hands,
Thy judgments are a mighty deep.   8

3. Thy providence is kind and large,
Both man and beaſt thy bounty ſhare;
The whole creation is thy charge,
But ſaints are thy peculiar care.   12

4. My God! how excellent thy grace!
Whence all our hope and comfort ſprings;
The ſons of Adam in diſtreſs
Fly to the ſhadow of thy wings.   16

5. From the proviſions of thy houſe
We ſhall be fed with ſweet repaſt,
There mercy like a river ſlows,
And brings ſalvation to our taſte.   20

6. Life like a fountain rich and free
Springs from the preſence of my Lord,
And in thy light our ſouls ſhall ſee
The glories promis'd in thy word.   24

PSALM XXXVI. ver, 1, 2, 5, 6, 7, 9. Common Metre.

Practical atheiſm expoſed, or, The being and attributes of God aſſerted.

WHILE men grow bold in wicked ways
And yet a God they own,
My heart within me often ſays
" Their thoughts believe there 's none."   4

Volume I.   N

2. Their thoughts and ways at once declare
(Whate'er their lips profefs)
God hath no wrath for them to fear,
Nor will they feek his grace.   8

3 What ftrange felf-flatt'ry blinds their eyes!
But there 's a haft'ning hour
When they fhall fee with fore furprife
The terrours of thy pow'r.   12

4. Thy juftice fhall maintain its throne
Tho' mountains melt away;
Thy judgments are a world unknown,
A deep unfathom'd fea.   16 .

5. Above thefe heav'ns' created rounds
Thy mercies Lord extend;
Thy truth outlives the narrow bounds
Where time and nature end.   20

6. Safety to man thy goodnefs brings,
Nor overlooks the beaft;
Beneath the fhadow of thy wings
Thy children chufe to reft.   24

[7. From thee when creature-ftreams run low
And mortal comforts die
Perpetual fprings of life fhall flow
And raife our pleafures high.   28

8. Tho' all created light decay
And death clofe up our eyes,
Thy prefence makes eternal day
Where clouds can never rife.]   32

PSALM XXXVI. ver. 1,—7. Short Metre.

The wickedness of man and the majesty of God, or, Prac-
tical atheism exposed.

WHEN man grows bold in sin
My heart within me cries,
" He hath no faith of God within
" Nor fear before his eyes."   4

[2. He walks a while conceal'd
In a self-flatt'ring dream,
Till his dark crimes at once reveal'd
Expose his hateful name.]   8

3. His heart is false and foul,
His words are smooth and fair,
Wisdom is banish'd from his soul
And leaves no goodness there.   12

4. He plots upon his bed
New mischiefs to fulfil;
He sets his heart, and hand, and head,
To practise all that 's ill.   16

5. But there 's a dreadful God
Tho' men renounce his fear,
His justice hid behind the cloud
Shall one great day appear   20

6. His truth transcends the sky,
In heav'n his mercies dwell,
Deep as the sea his judgments lie,
His anger burns to hell.   24

7. How excellent his love,
Whence all our safety springs!
O never let my foul remove
From underneath his wings!   28

PSALM XXXVII. ver. I,——15. First part.

The cure of envy, fretfulness, and unbelief, or, *The rewards of the righteous and the wicked,* or, *The world's
hatred and the saint's patience.*

Why should I vex my foul and fret
To fee the wicked rife,
Or envy finners waxing great
By violence and lies?   4
    2. As flow'ry grafs cut down at noon
Before the ev'ning fades,
So fhall their glories vanifh foon
In everlafting fhades.   8
    3. Then let me make the Lord my truft
And practife all that's good,
So fhall I dwell among the juft,
And he 'll provide me food.   12
    4. I to my God my ways commit
And cheerful wait his will;
Thy hand which guides my doubtful feet
Shall my defires fulfil.   16

5. Mine innocence fhalt thou difplay
And make thy judgments known,
Fair as the light of dawning day
And glorious as the noon.   20

6. The meek at laft the earth poffefs
And are the heirs of heav'n;
True riches with abundant peace
To humble fouls are giv'n.   24

PAUSE.

7. Reft in the Lord and keep his way,
Nor let your anger rife
Tho' Providence fhould long delay
To punifh haughty vice.   28

8. Let finners join to break your peace,
And plot, and rage, and foam,
The Lord derides them, for he fees
Their day of vengeance come.   32

9. They have drawn out the threat'ning fword,
Have bent the murd'rous bow,
To flay the men that fear the Lord,
And bring the righteous low.   36

10. My God fhall break their bows and burn
Their perfecuting darts,
Shall their own fwords againft them turp,
And pain furprife their hearts ‡.   40

‡ I have turned the divine inftructions at the beginning of
this Pfalm into the form of holy purpofes, as more affecting
and lively.

N iij

PSALM XXXVII. ver. 16, 21, 26,—31. Second part.

Charity to the poor, or, *Religion in words and deeds.*

Why do the wealthy wicked boast
And grow profanely bold?
The meanest portion of the just
Excels the sinner's gold.   4

2 The wicked borrows of his friends
But ne'er designs to pay,
The saint is merciful and lends,
Nor turns the poor away.   8

3. His alms with lib'ral heart he gives
Amongst the sons of need,
His mem'ry to long ages lives,
And blessed is his seed.   12

4. His lips abhor to talk profane,
To slander or defraud,
His ready tongue declares to men
What he has learn'd of God.   16

5. The law and gospel of the Lord
Deep in his heart abide;
Led by the Spirit and the Word
His feet shall never slide.   20

6. When sinners fall the righteous stand
Preserv'd from ev'ry snare;
They shall possess the promis'd land
And dwell for ever there.   24

PSALM XXXVII. ver. 23,—37. Third part.

The way and end of the righteous and wicked.

My God! the steps of pious men
Are order'd by thy will,
Tho' they should fall they rise again,
Thy hand supports them still.   4

  2. The Lord delights to see their ways,
Their virtue he approves;
He 'll ne'er deprive them of his grace
Nor leave the men he loves.   8

  3. The heav'nly heritage is theirs,
Their portion and their home;
He feeds them now, and makes them heirs
Of blessings long to come.   12

  4. Wait on the Lord ye sons of men!
Nor fear when tyrants frown;
Ye shall confess their pride was vain
When justice casts them down.   16

PAUSE.

  5. The haughty sinner have I seen
Nor fearing man nor God,
Like a tall baytree fair and green
Spreading his arms abroad;   20

  6. And lo! he vanish'd from the ground,
Destroy'd by hands unseen;
Nor root, nor branch, nor leaf, was found
Where all that pride had been.   24

7. But mark the man of rightcoufnefs,
His fev'ral fteps attend ;
True pleafure runs thro' all his ways,
And peaceful is hisend †.   28

PSALM XXXVIII.

Guilt of confcience and relief, or, Repentance and prayer for pardon and health.

Amidst thy wrath remember love,
Reftore thy fervant Lord,
Nor let a father's chaft'ning prove
Like an avenger's fword.   4

2. Thine arrows ftick within my heart,
My flefh is forely preft ;
Between the forrow and the fmart
My fpirit finds no reft.   o

3. My fins a heavy load appear,
And o'er my head are gone ;
Too heavy they for me to bear,
Too hard for me t' atone.   12

4. My thoughts are like a troubled fea,
My head ftill bending down,
And I go mourning all the day
Beneath my Father's frown.   16

† This long Pfalm abounds with ufeful Inftructions and encouragements to piety, but the verfes are very much unconnected and independent, therefore I have contracted and tranfpofed them fo as to reduce them to three hymns of a moderate length, and with fome connexion of the fenfe.

5. Lord I am weak and broken fore,
None of my pow'rs are whole,
The inward anguish makes me roar,
'The anguish of my foul. 20

6. All my defire to thee is known,
Thine eye counts ev'ry tear,
And ev'ry figh and ev'ry groan
Is notic'd by thine ear. 24

7. Thou art my God, my only hope,
My God will hear my cry,
My God will bear my fpirit up
When Satan bids me die. 28

[8. My foot is ever apt to flide,
My foes rejoice to fee 't;
They raife their pleafure and their pride
When they fupplant my feet. 32

9. But I 'll confefs my guilt to thee
And grieve for all my fin,
I 'll mourn how weak my graces be,
And beg fupport divine. 36

10. My God! forgive my follies paft,
And be for ever nigh;
O Lord of my falvation hafte
Before thy fervant die!] 40

PSALM XXXIX. ver. 1, 2, 3. First part.

Watchfulness over the tongue, or, *Prudence and zeal.*

Thus I resolv'd before the Lord,
" Now will I watch my tongue,
" Left I let flip one finful word
" Or do my neighbour wrong."   4
   2. And if I 'm e'er conftrain'd to ftay
With men of lives profane,
I 'll fet a double guard that day,
Nor let my talk be vain.   8
   3. I 'll fcarce allow my lips to fpeak
The pious thoughts I feel,
Left fcoffers fhould th' occafion take
T'o mock my holy zeal.   12
   4. Yet if fome proper hour appear
I 'll not be overaw'd,
But let the fcoffing finners hear
That we can fpeak for God ‡.   16

  ‡ I have not confined myfelf here to the fenfe of the Pfalmift, but have taken occafion from the three firft verfes to write a fhort hymn on the government of the tongue.

PSALM XXXIX. ver. 4, 5, 6, 7. Second part.

The vanity of man as mortal.

TEACH me the measure of my days,
Thou Maker of my frame!
I would survey life's narrow space,
And learn how frail I am.   4

  2. A span is all that we can boast,
An inch or two of time:
Man is but vanity and dust
In all his flow'r and prime.   8

  3. See the vain race of mortals move
Like shadows o'er the plain,
They rage and strive, desire and love,
But all the noise is vain.   12

  4. Some walk in honour's gaudy show,
Some dig for golden ore,
They toil for heirs they know not who,
And straight are seen no more.   16

  5. What should I wish or wait for then
From creatures earth and dust?
They make our expectations vain
And disappoint our trust.   20

  6. Now I forbid my carnal hope,
My fond desires recall,
I give my mortal int'rest up,
And make my God my all.   24

PSALM XXXIX. ver. 9,—13. Third part.

Sickled devotion, or, *Pleading without repining.*

God of my life look gently down,
Behold the pains I feel;
But I am dumb before thy throne,
Nor dare difpute thy will.   4

2. Difeafes are thy fervants Lord,
They come at thy command;
I 'll not attempt a murm'ring word
Againft thy chaft'ning hand.   8

3. Yet I may plead with humble cries
Remove thy fharp rebukes:
My ftrength confumes my fpirit dies
Thro' thy repeated ftrokes.   12

4. Crufh'd as a moth beneath thy hand
We moulder to the duft:
Our feeble pow'rs can ne'er withftand,
And all our beauty's loft.   16

[5. This mortal life decays apace,
How foon the bubble's broke!
Adam and all his num'rous race
Are vanity and fmoke.]   20

6. I 'm but a fojourner below
As all my fathers were;
May I be well prepar'd to go
When I the fummons hear.   24

4

7. But if my life be spar'd a while
Before my laft remove,
Thy praife fhall be my bus'nefs ftill,
And I 'll declare thy love.   28

PSALM XL. ver. 1, 2, 3, ɛ,—17. Firft Part.
Common Metre.

A fong of deliverance from great diftrefs.

I Waited patient for the Lord,
He bow'd to hear my cry,
He faw me retling on his word
And brought falvation nigh.   4

2. He rais'd me from a horrid pit
Where mourning long I lay,
And from my bonds releas'd my feet,
Deep bonds of miry clay.   8

3. Firm on a rock he made me ftand,
And taught my cheerful tongue
To praife the wonders of his hand
In a new thankful fong.   12

4. I 'll fpread his works of grace abroad;
The faints with joy fhall hear,
And finners learn to make my God
Their only hope and fear.   16

5. How many are thy thoughts of love,
Thy mercies Lord how great!
We have not words nor hours enough
Their numbers to repeat.   20

6. When I 'm afflicted, poor, and low,
And light and peace depart,
My God beholds my heavy wo
And bears me on his heart.   24

PSALM XL. ver. 6,—9. Second part. Common Metre.

The incarnation and sacrifice of Christ.

Thus saith the Lord, " Your work is vain,
" Give your burnt off'rings o'er,
" In dying goats and bullocks slain
" My soul delights no more."   4
    2. Then spake the Saviour, " Lo I 'm here
" My God to do thy will;
" Whate'er thy sacred books declare
" Thy servant shall fulfil.   8
    3. " Thy law is ever in my sight,
" I keep it near my heart;
" Mine ears are open'd with delight
" To what thy lips impart."   12
    4. And see! the bless'd Redeemer comes,
Th' Eternal Son appears,
And at th' appointed time assumes
The body God prepares.   16
    5. Much he reveal'd his Father's grace,
And much his truth he shew'd,
And preach'd the way of righteousness
Where great assemblies stood.   20

6. His Father's honour touch'd his heart,
He pity'd sinners' cries,
And to fulfil a Saviour's part
Was made a sacrifice.   24

PAUSE.

7. No blood of beasts on altars shed
Could wash the conscience clean,
But the rich sacrifice he paid
Atones for all our sin.   28

8. Then was the great salvation spread,
And Satan's kingdom shook :
Thus by the woman's promis'd seed
The serpent's head was broke ‡.   32

‡ If David had written this Psalm in the days of the gospel
surely he would have given a much more express and particular account of the sacrifice of Christ, as he hath done of his
preaching, ver. 9. 10. and enlarged as Paul does in *Heb.* x.
4, &c. where this Psalm is cited. I have done no more therefore in this paraphrase than what I am persuaded the Psalmist
himself would have done in the time of Christianity.—The
scriptures which I have used here on this occasion are, Heb. x.
4. *It is not possible the blood of bulls and of goats should take away
sin ;* ver. 5. *A body hast thou prepared me ;* John vii. 18. *I seek
the glory of him that sent me ;* Heb. x. 26. *He appeared to put
away sin by the sacrifice of himself ;* Gen. iii. 15. *The seed of the
woman shall bruise the serpent's head.*

O ij

PSALM XL. ver. 5,—10. Long Metre.

Christ our sacrifice.

THE wonders Lord! thy love has wrought
Exceed our praise, surmount our thought;
Should I attempt the long detail
My speech would faint my numbers fail.

2. No blood of beasts on altars spilt
Can cleanse the souls of men from guilt,
But thou hast set before our eyes
An allsufficient sacrifice.

3. Lo thine eternal Son appears,
To thy designs he bows his ears,
Assumes a body will prepar'd,
And well performs a work so hard.

4. " Behold I come," the Saviour cries,
With love and duty in his eyes;
" I come to bear the heavy load
" Of sins, and do thy will my God.

5. " 'Tis written in thy great decree,
" 'Tis in thy book foretold of me,
" I must fulfil the Saviour's part,
" And lo thy law is in my heart.

6. " I 'll magnify thy holy law,
" And rebels to obedience draw,
" When on my cross I 'm lifted high,
" Or to my crown above the sky.

7. " The Spirit fhall defcend and fhow
" What thou haft done and what I do;.
" The wond'ring world fhall learn thy grace,
" Thy wifdom and thy righteoufnefs ‡." 28

PSALM XLI. ver. I, 2, 3.

Charity to the poor, or, *Pity to the afflicted.*

BLESS'D is the man whofe bowels move
And melt with pity to the poor,
Whofe foul by fympathizing love
Feels what his fellow faints endure. 4

2. His heart contrives for their relief
More good than his own hands can do;
He in the time of gen'ral grief
Shall find the Lord has bowels too. 8

3. His foul fhall live fecure on earth
With fecret bleffings on his head
When drought, and peftilence, and dearth,
Around him multiply their dead. 12

‡ Befides fome of the fcriptures mentioned under the former
metre I have here made ufe of thefe alfo, 1 *Joh*. iii. 5. *The Son of
God was manifefted*, &c. ; 1 Pet. ii. 24. *He bare our fins* ; Ifa.
xlii. 21. *He will magnify the law and make it honourable* ;
John xii. 32. *If I be lifted up I will draw all men to me* ; John
xvi. 14. *The Spirit fhall receive of mine and fhew it unto you.*

O iij

4. Or if he languish on his couch
God will pronounce his sins forgiv'n,
Will save him with a healing touch,
Or take his willing soul to heav'n ‡.   16

PSALM XLII. ver. 1,—5. The first part.

Desertion and hope, or, *Complaint of absence from publick*
worship.

WITH earnest longings of the mind
My God to thee I look;
So pants the hunted hart to find
And taste the cooling brook.   4

2. When shall I see thy courts of grace
And meet my God again?
So long an absence from thy face
My heart endures with pain.   8

3. Temptations vex my weary soul,
And tears are my repast;
The foe insults without control,
" And where 's your God at last?"   12

‡ The ten last verses of this Psalm are of quite another subject, relating to David's personal enemies, which being so frequently repeated I have often omitted.--The positive blessings
of long life, health, recovery, and security, in the midst of
dangers, being so much promised in The Old Testament, and
so little in The New, I have given a turn at the end of this hymn
to discourage a too confident expectation of these temporal
things, and led the soul to heavenly hopes more agreeable to
the gospel.

4. 'Tis with a mournful pleafure now
I think on ancient days,
Then to thy houfe did numbers go,
And all our work was praife.   16

5. But why my foul funk down fo far
Beneath this heavy load?
Why do my thoughts indulge defpair
And fin againft my God?   20

6. Hope in the Lord, whofe mighty hand
Can all thy woes remove,
For I fhall yet before him ftand
And fing reftoring love.   24

PSALM XLII. ver. 6,—11. The fecond part.

Melancholy thoughts reproved, or, Hope in afflictions.

My fpirit finks within me Lord,
But I will call thy name to mind,
And times of paft diftrefs record,
When I have found my God was kind.   4

2. Huge troubles with tumultuous noife
Swell like a fea and round me fprend;
Thy waterfpouts drown all my joys,
And rifing waves roll o'er my head.   8

3. Yet will the Lord command his love
When I addrefs his throne by day,
Nor in the night his grace remove,
The night fhall hear me fing and pray.   12

4. I 'll caft myfelf before his feet,
And fay, " My God, my heav'nly Rock!
" Why doth thy love fo long forget
" The foul that groans beneath thy ftroke?"   16

5. I 'll chide my heart that finks fo low;
Why fhould my foul indulge her grief?
Hope in the Lord and praife him too;
He is my reft, my fure relief.   20

6. Thy light and truth fhall guide me ftill,
Thy word fhall my beft thoughts employ,
And lead me to thine heav'nly hill,
My God, my moft exceeding joy ‡!   24

PSALM XLIV. ver. 1, 2, 3, 8, 15,—26.

The church's complaint in perfecution.

LORD we have heard thy works of old,
Thy works of pow'r and grace,
When to our ears our fathers told
The wonders of their days;   4

2. How thou didft build thy churches here
And make thy gofpel known;
Amongft them did thine arm appear,
Thy light and glory fhone.   8

‡ The xliiid Pfalm is fo near akin to this that I have omitted it, only borrowing the 3d and 4th verfes to conclude this hymn.

3. In God they boasted all the day,
And in a cheerful throng
Did thousands meet to praise and pray,
And grace was all their song.   12

4. But now our souls are seiz'd with shame,
Confusion fills our face,
To hear the enemy blaspheme,
And fools reproach thy grace.   16

5. Yet have we not forgot our God,
Nor falsely dealt with Heav'n,
Nor have our steps declin'd the road
Of duty thou hast giv'n;   20

6. Tho' dragons all around us roar
With their destructive breath,
And thine own hand has bruis'd us sore
Hard by the gates of death.   24

PAUSE.

7. We are expos'd all day to die
As martyrs for thy cause,
As sheep for slaughter bound we lie
By sharp and bloody laws.   28

8. Awake, arise, almighty Lord!
Why sleeps thy wonted grace?   .. .
Why should we look like men abhorr'd
Or banish'd from thy face?   32

9. Wilt thou for ever cast us off
And still neglect our cries,
For ever hide thine heav'nly love
From our afflicted eyes?   .. .   36

10. Down to the duſt our ſoul is bow'd,
And dies upon the ground;
Riſe for our help, rebuke the proud,
And all their pow'rs confound.   40

11. Redeem us from perpetual ſhame
Our Saviour and our God;
We plead the honours of thy name,
The merits of thy blood.   44

PSALM XLV. Short Metre.

*The glory of Chriſt, the ſucceſs of the goſpel, and the Gentile
church.*

My Saviour and my King
Thy beauties are divine;
Thy lips with bleſſings overflow,
And ev'ry grace is thine.   4

2. Now make thy glory known,
Gird on thy dreadful ſword,
And ride in majeſty to ſpread
The conqueſts of thy word.   8

3. Strike thro' thy ſtubborn foes,
Or melt their hearts t' obey,
While juſtice, meekneſs, grace and truth,
Attend thy glorious way.   12

4. Thy laws O God are right,
Thy throne ſhall ever ſtand,
And thy victorious goſpel proves
A ſceptre in thy hand.   :   16

[5. Thy Father and thy God
Hath without meafure fhed
His Spirit like a joyful oil
T' anoint thy facred head.]   20

[6. Behold at thy right hand
The Gentile church is feen
Like a fair bride in rich attire,
And princes guard the queen.]   24

7. Fair bride receive his love,
Forget thy father's houfe,
Forfake thy gods, thy idol gods,
And pay thy Lord thy vows.   28

8. O let thy God and King
Thy fweeteft thoughts employ,
Thy children fhall his honours fing
In palaces of joy †.   32

PSALM XLV. Common Metre.

The perfonal glories and government of Chrift.

I 'll fpeak the honours of my King;
His form divinely fair,
None of the fons of mortal race
May with the Lord compare.   4

---

† This Pfalm is a defcription of the perfonal glories of Chrift
and the fuccefs of his gofpel, and probably it refers to the Gentile church, becaufe fhe is bid to *forget her father's houfe*, all
under the type of Solomon's marriage to Pharaoh's daughter.
—Stanza v. John iii. 34. *God giveth not the fpirit by meafure
unto him.*

2. Sweet is thy speech, and heav'nly grace
Upon thy lips is shed;
Thy God with blessings infinite
Hath crown'd thy sacred head.   8

3. Gird on thy sword victorious Prince,
Ride with majestick sway,
Thy terrours shall strike thro' thy foes
And make the world obey.   12

4. Thy throne O God for ever stands;
Thy word of grace shall prove
A peaceful sceptre in thy hands
To rule the saints by love.   16

5. Justice and truth attend thee still,
But mercy is thy choice;
And God thy God thy soul shall fill
With most peculiar joys.   20

PSALM XLV. The first part. Long Metre.

The glory of Christ and power of his gospel.

Now be my heart inspir'd to sing
The glories of my Saviour King,
Jesus the Lord; how heav'nly fair
His form! how bright his beauties are!   4

2. O'er all the sons of human race
He shines with a superiour grace,
Love from his lips divinely flows,
And blessings all his state compose.   8

3. Dreſs thee in arms moſt mighty Lord!
Gird on the terrour of thy ſword,
In majeſty and glory ride
With truth and meekneſs at thy ſide.   12

4. Thine anger like a pointed dart
Shall pierce the foes of ſtubborn heart,
Or words of mercy kind and ſweet
Shall melt the rebels at thy feet.   16

5. Thy throne O God for ever ſtands,
Grace is the ſceptre in thy hands ;
Thy laws and works are juſt and right,
Juſtice and grace are thy delight.   20

6. God thine own God has richly ſhed
His oil of gladneſs on thy head,
And with his ſacred Spirit bleſt
His firſt-born Son above the reſt.   24

PSALM XLV. Second part. Long Metre.

Chriſt and his church, or, *The myſtical marriage.*

THE King of ſaints how fair his face,
Adorn'd with majeſty and grace!
He comes with bleſſings from above
And wins the nations to his love.   4

2. At his right hand our eyes behold
The queen array'd in pureſt gold,
The world admires her heav'nly dreſs,
Her robe of joy and righteouſneſs.   8

Volume I.   P

3. He form'd her beauties like his own,
He calls and feats her near his throne:
Fair stranger let thine heart forget
The idols of thy native state.   12

4 So shall the King the more rejoice
In thee the fav'rite of his choice:
Let him be lov'd and yet ador'd,
For he 's thy Maker and thy Lord.   16

5. O happy hour when thou shalt rise
To his fair palace in the skies,
And all his sons (a num'rous train)
Each like a prince in glory reign.   20

6. Let endless honours crown his head,
Let ev'ry age his praises spread,
While we with cheerful songs approve
The condescensions of his love ‡.   24

PSALM XLVI. First part.

The church's safety and triumph among national desolations.

God is the refuge of his saints
When storms of sharp distress invade;
Ere we can offer our complaints
Behold him present with his aid.   4

2. Let mountains from their seats be hurl'd
Down to the deep and bury'd there,
Convulsions shake the solid world,
Our faith shall never yield to fear.   8

‡ See the Notes on the short metre.

3. Loud may the troubled ocean roar,
In sacred peace our souls abide
While ev'ry nation ev'ry shore
Trembles, and dreads the swelling tide.   12

4. There is a stream whose gentle flow
Supplies the city of our God,
Life, love, and joy, still gliding thro',
And wat'ring our divine abode.   16

5. That sacred stream thine Holy Word,
That all our raging fear controls:
Sweet peace thy promises afford,
And give new strength to fainting souls.   20

6. Sion enjoys her Monarch's love,
Secure against a threat'ning hour,
Nor can her firm foundations move,
Built on his truth and arm'd with pow'r.   24

PSALM XLVI. Second part.

God fights for his church.

L . . . in her King rejoice
Tho' . . s rage and kingdoms rise;
He utte . . almighty voice,
The nati . . . melt, the tumult dies.   4

2. Th . . . of old for Jacob fought,
And J . . God is still our aid;
Beho . . works his hand has wrought,
Wh . . lations he has made.   8

P ij

3. From fea to fea thro' all the fhores
He makes the noife of battle ceafe;
When from on high his thunder roars
He awes the trembling world to peace.　　　12

4. He breaks the bow, he cuts the fpear,
Chariots he burns with heav'nly flame;
Keep filence all the earth, and hear
The found and glory of his name.　　　16

5. " Be ftill, and learn that I am God,
" I 'll be exalted o'er the lands,
" I will be known and fear'd abroad,
" But ftill my throne in Sion ftands."　　　20

6. O Lord of hofts, almighty King!
While we fo near thy prefence dwell
Our faith fhall fit fecure, and fing
Defiance to the gates of hell.　　　24

PSALM XLVII.

Chrift afcending and reigning.

O For a fhout of facred joy
To God the fov'reign King!
Let ev'ry land their tongues employ
And hymns of triumph fing.　　　4

2. Jefus our God afcends on high;
His heav'nly guards around
Attend him rifing thro' the fky
With trumpets' joyful found.　　　8

3. While angels shout and praise their King
Let mortals learn their strains:
Let all the earth his honour sing;
O'er all the earth he reigns.   12

4. Rehearse his praise with awe profound,
Let knowledge lead the song,
Nor mock him with a solemn sound
Upon a thoughtless tongue.   16

5. In Israel stood his ancient throne,
He lov'd that chosen race,
But now he calls the world his own,
And Heathens taste his grace.   20

6. The British islands are the Lord's,
There Abra'm's God is known,
While pow'rs and princes shields and swords
Submit before his throne †.   24

PSALM XLVIII. ver. 1,—8. The first part.

The church is the honour and safety of a nation.

[GREAT is the Lord our God,
And let his praise be great,
He makes his churches his abode,
His most delightful seat.   4

† The ascent of Christ into heaven is typified in this Psalm by
the ark brought up to Sion, 2 Sam. vi. 15.; and the kingdom
of Christ among the Gentiles is here represented by David's
victory over the nations, ver. 3. I have chosen to omit the
type, and do honour to my ascending and reigning Saviour in
more express language.

2. Thefe temples of his grace
How beautiful they ftand!
The honours of our native place,
And bulwarks of our land.]   8

3. In Sion God is known
A refuge in diftrefs;
How bright has his falvation fhone
Thro' all her palaces!   12

4. When kings againft her join'd,
And faw the Lord was there,
In wild confufion of the mind
They fled with hafty fear.   16

5. When navies tall and proud
Attempt to fpoil our peace,
He fends his tempeft roaring loud
And finks them in the feas.   20

6. Oft' have our fathers told,
Our eyes have often feen,
How well our God fecures the fold
Where his own fheep have been.   24

7. In ev'ry new diftrefs
We 'll to his houfe repair,
We 'll think upon his wondrous grace
And feek deliv'rance there.   28

PSALM XLVIII. ver. 10,—14. The second part.

The beauty of the church, or, *Gospel-worship and order.*

FAR as thy name is known
The world declares thy praise,
Thy faints O Lord before thy throne
Their fongs of honour raife.   4

   2. With joy let Judah ſtand
On Sion's chofen hill,
Proclaim the wonders of thy hand
And counfels of thy will.   8

   3. Let ſtrangers walk around
The city where we dwell,
Compaſs and view thine holy ground,
And mark the building well;   12

   4. The orders of thy houſe,
The worſhip of thy court,
The cheerful fongs, the folemn vows,
And make a fair report.   16

   5. How decent and how wife,
How glorious to behold!
Beyond the pomp that charms the eyes,
And rites adorn'd with gold.   20

   6. The God we worſhip now
Will guide us till we die,
Will be our God while here below,
And ours above the ſky.   24

PSALM XLIX. ver. 6,—14. First part.
Common Metre.

Pride and death, or, *The vanity of life and riches.*

Why doth the man of riches grow
To infolence and pride,
To fee his wealth and honours flow
With ev'ry rifing tide ?   4

[2. Why doth he treat the poor with fcorn,
Made of the felffame clay,
And boaft as tho' his flefh was born
Of better duft than they ?]   8

3. Not all his treafures can procure
His foul a fhort reprieve,
Redeem from death one guilty hour,
Or make his brother live.   12

[4. Life is a bleffing cann't be fold,
The ranfom is too high;
Juftice will ne'er be brib'd with gold
That man may never die.]   16

5. He fees the brutifh and the wife,
The tim'rous and the brave,
Quit their poffeffions, clofe their eyes,
And haften to the grave.   20

6. Yet 't is his inward thought and pride
" My houfe fhall ever ftand,
" And that my name may long abide
" I 'll give it to my land."   24

7. Vain are his thoughts, his hopes are loſt,
How ſoon his mem'ry dies!
His name is written in the duſt
Where his own carcaſs lies.   28

8. This is the folly of their way,
And yet their ſons as vain
Approve the words their fathers ſay
And act their works again.   32

9. Men void of wiſdom and of grace,
If honour raiſe them high,
Live like the beaſt, a thoughtleſs race,
And like the beaſt they die.   36

10. Laid in the grave like ſilly ſheep
Death feeds upon them there,
Till the laſt trumpet breaks their ſleep
In terrour and deſpair.   40

PSALM XLIX. ver. 14, 15. Second part.
Common Metre.

Death and the reſurrection.

YE ſons of pride that hate the juſt
And trample on the poor,
When death has brought you down to duſt
Your pomp ſhall riſe no more.   4

2. The laſt great day ſhall change the ſcene;
When will that hour appear?
When ſhall the juſt revive and reign
O'er all that ſcorn'd them here?   8

3. God will my naked ſoul receive
When ſep'rate from the fleſh,
And break the priſon of the grave
To raiſe my bones afreſh.   12

4. Heav'n is my everlaſting home,
Th' inheritance is ſure;
Let men of pride their rage reſume,
But I 'll repine no more.   16

PSALM XLIX. Long Metre.

The rich ſinner's death and the ſaint's reſurrection.

Why do the proud inſult the poor,
And boaſt the large eſtates they have?
How vain are riches to ſecure
Their haughty owners from the grave!   :   4

2. They cann't redeem one hour from death
With all the wealth in which they truſt,
Nor give a dying brother breath
When God commands him down to duſt.   8

3. There the dark earth and diſmal ſhade
Shall claſp their naked bodies round,
That fleſh ſo delicately fed
Lies cold and moulders in the ground.   . . 12

4. Like thoughtlefs fheep the finner dies,
Laid in the grave for worms to eat;
The faints fhall in the morning rife
And find th' oppreffor at their feet.   16

5. His honours perifh in the duft,
And pomp, and beauty, birth, and blood;
That glorious day exalts the juft
To full dominion o'er the proud.   20

6. My Saviour fhall my life reftore
And raife me from my dark abode;
My flefh and foul fhall part no more
But dwell for ever near my God.   24

PSALM L. ver. 1,—6. Firft part. Common Metre.

The laft judgment, or, *The faints rewarded.*

Tue Lord the Judge before his throne
Bids the whole earth draw nigh,
The nations near the rifing fun
And near the weftern fky.   4

2. No more fhall bold blafphemers fay
" Judgment will near begin,"
No more abufe his long delay
To impudence and fin.   8

3. Thron'd on a cloud our God fhall come,
Bright flames prepare his way,
Thunder and darknefs, fire and ftorm,
Lead on the dreadful day.   12

4. Heav'n from above his call shall hear,
Attending angels come,
And earth and hell shall know and fear
His justice and their doom.   16

  5 " But gather all my saints," he cries,
" That made their peace with God
" By the Redeemer's sacrifice,
" And seal'd it with his blood.   20

  6. " Their faith and works brought forth to light
" Shall make the world confess
" My sentence of reward is right,
" And heav'n adore my grace."   24

PSALM L. ver. 8, 10, 11, 14, 15, 23. Second part.
Common Metre.

Obedience is better than sacrifice.

Thus saith the Lord, " The spacious fields,
" And flocks and herds, are mine;
" O'er all the cattle of the hills
" I claim a right divine.   4

  2. " I ask no sheep for sacrifice,
" Nor bullocks burnt with fire;
" To hope and love, to pray and praise,
" Is all that I require.   8

  3. " Call upon me when trouble 's near,
" My hand shall set thee free,
" Then shall thy thankful lips declare
" The honour due to me.   12

    5

4. " The man that offers humble praise
" He glorifies me best,
" And those that tread my holy ways
" Shall my salvation taste." 16

PSALM L. ver. 1, 5, 8, 16, 21, 22. Third part.
Common Metre.

The judgment of hypocrites.

WHEN Christ to judgment shall descend
And saints surround their Lord,
He calls the nations to attend
And hear his awful word. 4

2. " Not for the want of bullocks slain
" Will I the world reprove;
" Altars, and rites, and forms, are vain
" Without the fire of love. 8

3. " And what have hypocrites to do
" To bring their sacrifice?
" They call my statutes just and true
" But deal in theft and lies. 12

4. " Could you expect to 'scape my sight
" And sin without control?
" But I shall bring your crimes to light
" With anguish in your soul." 16

5. Consider ye that slight the Lord
Before his wrath appear;
If once you fall beneath his sword
There's no deliv'rer there. 20

Volume I. Q

PSALM L. Third part. Long Metre.

Hypocrisy exposed.

The Lord the Judge his churches warns;
Let hypocrites attend and fear
Who place their hopes in rites and forms
But make not faith nor love their care.   4

2. Vile wretches dare rehearse his name
With lips of falsehood and deceit;
A friend or brother they defame,
And sooth and flatter those they hate.   8

3. They watch to do their neighbours wrong,
Yet dare to seek their Maker's face;
They take his cov'nant on their tongue
But break his laws, abuse his grace.   12

4. To Heav'n they lift their hands unclean,
Defil'd with lust, defil'd with blood;
By night they practise ev'ry sin,
By day their mouths draw near to God.   16

5. And while his judgments long delay
They grow secure and sin the more;
They think he sleeps as well as they,
And put far off the dreadful hour.   20

6. O dreadful hour! when God draws near
And sets their crimes before their eyes!
His wrath their guilty souls shall tear,
And no deliv'rer dare to rise †.   24

† This Psalm having a plain reference to the last judgment
I have in the first part omitted every thing that might obscure

PSALM L. To a new tune.

The last judgment.

THE Lord the Sov'reign sends his summons forth,
Calls the south nations and awakes the north,
From east to west the sounding orders spread
Thro' distant worlds and regions of the dead:
No more shall atheists mock his long delay;
His vengeance sleeps no more: behold the day!   6

2. Behold the Judge descends! his guards are nigh,
Tempest and fire attend him down the sky:
Heav'n, earth, and hell, draw near; let all things come
To hear his justice and the sinner's doom:
But gather first my saints the Judge commands,
Bring them ye angels from their distant lands.   12

3. Behold my cov'nant stands for ever good,
Seal'd by th' eternal sacrifice in blood;
And sign'd with all their names; the Greek, the Jew,
That paid the ancient worship or the new:
There's no distinction here: come. spread their thrones,
And near me seat my fav'rites and my sons.   18

4. I their almighty Saviour and their God,
I am their Judge: ye heav'ns proclaim abroad

the sense of it.——The latter part of this Psalm being designed
to expose and terrify all formal worshippers and hypocrites, I
have formed two or three hymns on that subject with some
transposition and paraphrase of the verses. but I have kept the
same introduction still by repeating the first verse of the Psalm.

My juſt eternal ſentence, and declare
Thoſe awful truths that ſinners dread to hear:
Sinners in Sion tremble and retire,
I doom the painted hypocrite to fire.   24

    5. Not for the want of goats or bullocks ſlain
Do I condemn thee; bulls and goats are vain
Without the flames of love; in vain the ſtore
Of brutal off'rings that were mine before:
Mine are the tamer beaſts and ſavage breed,
Flocks, herds, and fields, and foreſts where they feed.

    6. If I were hungry would I aſk thee food?   31
When did I thirſt or drink thy bullocks' blood?
Can I be flatter'd with thy cringing bows,
Thy ſolemn chatt'rings and fantaſtick vows?   .
Are my eyes charm'd thy veſtments to behold
Glaring in gems and gay in woven gold?   36

    7. Unthinking wretch! how couldſt thou hope to
A God, a Spirit, with ſuch toys as theſe,   [pleaſe
While with my grace and ſtatutes on thy tongue
Thou lov'ſt deceit and doſt thy brother wrong?
In vain to pious forms thy zeal pretends,   .
Thieves and adult'rers are thy choſen friends.   42

    8. Silent I waited with long-ſuff'ring love,
But didſt thou hope that I ſhould ne'er reprove?
And cheriſh ſuch an impious thought within
That God the righteous would indulge thy ſin?
Behold my terrours now; my thunders roll,
And thy own crimes affright thy guilty ſoul.   48

9. Sinners awake betimes, ye fools be wise,
Awake before this dreadful morning rise,   [mend,
Change your vain thoughts, your crooked works a-
Fly to the Saviour, make the Judge your friend,
Lest like a lion his last vengeance tear, .' .
Your trembling souls, and no deliv'rer near ‡.   54

PSALM L. To the old proper tune. ·

The last judgment.

THE God of glory sends his summons forth,
Calls the south nations and awakes the north,
From east to west the sov'reign orders spread
Thro' distant worlds and regions of the dead :
The trumpet sounds, hell trembles, heav'n rejoices,
Lift up your heads ye saints with cheerful voices.   6
2. No more shall atheists mock his long delay;
His vengeance sleeps no more : behold the day!

‡ In this metre, as in some of the former, I have taken evident occasion from this Psalm to represent the last judgment,
and have therefore left out those verses that seem to interrupt
that sense.—Stanza iii. All the *saints have made a covenant
with God by sacrifice,* (as in the text) and as it were set their
names to God's covenant of grace, ratified by the sacrifice of
Christ of eternal virtue, though the Jews did it in the ancient
forms of worship, and the Gentiles in the new.—Stanza vj, vii.
As the Jewish formal worshippers contented themselves with
burnt-offerings, &c. and trusted in them, so hypocrites in
Christianity build their hopes upon outward forms, gay cere-
monies, rigid austerities, fanciful vows, &c.

Q iij

Behold the Judge defcends! his guards are nigh,
Tempeſts and fire attend him down the ſky :
When God appears all nature ſhall adore him ;
While finners tremble faints rejoice before him.　12

　3. " Heav'n, earth, and hell, draw near; let all things
" To hear my juſtice and the finner's doom :　[come
" But gather firſt my faints," the Judge commands,
" Bring them ye angels from their diſtant lands."
When Chriſt returns wake ev'ry cheerful paſſion,
And ſhout ye faints; he comes for your falvation. 18

　4. " Behold my cov'nant ſtands for ever good,
" Seal'd by th' eternal facrifice in blood,
" And fign'd with all their names ; the Greek, the Jew,
" That paid the ancient worſhip or the new :"
There 's no diſtinction here; join all your voices,
And raife your heads ye faints, for Heav'n rejoices. 24

　5. " Here," faith the Lord, " ye angels ſpread their
　　　. thrones,
" And near me feat my fav'rites and my fons :
" Come my redeem'd, poſſefs the joys prepar'd
" Ere time began, 't is your divine reward."
When Chriſt returns wake ev'ry cheerful paſſion,
And ſhout ye faints; he comes for your falvation.　30

PAUSE THE FIRST.

　6. " I am the Saviour, I th' almighty God,
" I am the Judge ; ye heav'ns proclaim abroad
" My juſt eternal fentence, and declare
" Thofe awful truths that finners dread to hear."

　2

When God appears all nature shall adore him;
While sinners tremble saints rejoice before him. 36

7. "Stand forth thou bold blasphemer and profane,
"Now feel my wrath, nor call my threat'nings vain
"Thou hypocrite, once dress'd in saints' attire;
"I doom the painted hypocrite to fire."
Judgment proceeds, hell trembles, heav'n rejoices,
Lift up your heads ye saints with cheerful voices. 42

8. "Not for the want of goats or bullocks slain
"Do I condemn thee; bulls and goats are in vain
"Without the flames of love; in vain the store
"Of brutal off'rings that were mine before:"
Earth is the Lord's, all nature shall adore him;
While sinners tremble saints rejoice before him. 48

9. "If I were hungry would I ask thee food?
"When did I thirst or drink thy bullocks' blood?
"Mine are the tamer beasts and savage breed, [feed:"
"Flocks, herds, and fields, and forests where they
All is the Lord's, he rules the wide creation,
Gives sinners vengeance and the saints salvation. 54

10. "Can I be flatter'd with thy cringing bows,
"Thy solemn chatt'rings and fantastick vows?
"Are my eyes charm'd thy vestments to behold
"Glaring in gems and gay in woven gold?"
God is the judge of hearts: no fair disguises
Can screen the guilty when his vengeance rises. 60

PAUSE THE SECOND.

11. "Unthinking wretch! how couldſt thou hope
" A God, a Spirit, with ſuch toys as theſe, [to pleaſe
" While with my grace and ſtatutes on thy tongue
" Thou lov'ſt deceit and doſt thy brother wrong?"
Judgment proceeds, hell trembles, heav'n rejoices,
Lift up your heads ye ſaints with cheerful voices. 66

12. "In vain to pious forms thy zeal pretends,
" Thieves and adult'rers are thy choſen friends:
" While the falſe flatt'rer at my altar waits
" His harden'd ſoul divine inſtruction hates."
God is the judge of hearts; no fair diſguiſes
Can ſcreen the guilty when his vengeance riſes. 72

13. "Silent I waited with long-ſuff'ring love,
" But didſt thou hope that I ſhould ne'er reprove?
" And cheriſh ſuch an impious thought within
" That the All-holy would indulge thy ſin?"
See God appears, all nations join t' adore him,
Judgment proceeds, and ſinners fall before him. 78

14. "Behold my terrours now; my thunders roll,
" And thy own crimes affright thy guilty ſoul;
" Now like a lion ſhall my vengeance tear
" Thy bleeding heart and no deliv'rer near."
Judgment concludes, hell trembles, heav'n rejoices,
Lift up your heads ye ſaints with cheerful voices. 84

EPIPHONEMA.

Sinners awake betimes, ye fools be wise,
Awake before this dreadful morning rise, [amend,
Change your vain thoughts, your crooked works
Fly to the Saviour, make the Judge your friend;
Then join ye saints, wake ev'ry cheerful passion,
When Christ returns he comes for your salvation †. 90

PSALM LI. The first part. Long Metre.

A penitent pleading for pardon.

SHEW pity Lord, O Lord forgive!
Let a repenting rebel live:
Are not thy mercies large and free?
May not a sinner trust in thee?   4

2. My crimes are great, but not surpass
The pow'r and glory of thy grace:
Great God! thy nature hath no bound,
So let thy pard'ning love be found.   8

3. O wash my soul from ev'ry sin,
And make my guilty conscience clean!
Here on my heart the burden lies,
And past offences pain mine eyes.   12

† If the former heroick metre do not fit the old proper tune
of the 50th Psalm for want of double rhymes at the end of
every stanza, I have here altered the form of it much in order to fit it exactly to the proper tune, adding a chorus, or
(as some call it) the burden of the song betwixt every four
lines. I hope it will not be displeasing to the more musical part
of my readers to be entertained with such a variety.

4. My lips with shame my sins confess
Against thy law, against thy grace;
Lord should thy judgment grow severe
I am condemn'd but thou art clear.   16

5. Should sudden vengeance seize my breath
I must pronounce thee just in death,
And if my soul were sent to hell
Thy righteous law approves it well.   20

6. Yet save a trembling sinner Lord,
Whose hope still hov'ring round thy word
Would light on some sweet promise there,
Some sure support, against despair.   24

PSALM LI. The second part. Long Metre.

Original and actual sin confessed.

LORD I am vile, conceiv'd in sin,
And born unholy and unclean,
Sprung from the man whose guilty fall
Corrupts the race and taints us all.   4

2. Soon as we draw our infant breath
The seeds of sin grow up for death:
Thy law demands a perfect heart,
But we 're defil'd in ev'ry part.   8

[3. Great God! create my heart anew,
And form my spirit pure and true;
O make me wise betimes to spy
My danger and my remedy.]   12

4. Behold I fall before thy face;
My only refuge is thy grace:
No outward forms can make me clean,
The leprofy lies deep within. 16

5. No bleeding bird nor bleeding beaft,
Nor hyffop branch nor fprinkling prieft,
Nor running brook, nor flood, nor fea,
Can wafh the difmal ftain away. 20

6. Jefus my God! thy blood alone
Hath pow'r fufficient to atone;
Thy blood can make me white as fnow;
No Jewifh types could cleanfe me fo. 24

7. While guilt difturbs and breaks my peace,
Nor flefh nor foul hath reft or eafe,
Lord let me hear thy pard'ning voice,
And make my broken bones rejoice *. 28

PSALM LI. The third part. Long Metre.

*The backflider reftored, or, Repentance and faith in the blead
of Chrift.*

O Thou that hear'ft when finners cry,
Tho' all my crimes before thee lie
Behold them not with angry look,
But blot their mem'ry from thy book. 4

---

* Stanza iv, v. Since the Pfalmift feems to refer to the *branch of hyffop, fprinkling the blood of the bird, and the running water*, Levit. xiv. 51. I have here enlarged upon the infufficiency of all thofe rites for the cleanfing of fin, which is the leprofy of the foul.—Stanza vi. Such a glorious occafion of introducing the blood of a Saviour could not be omitted here with juftice to David or to Chrift his fon.

2. Create my nature pure within,
And form my soul averse to sin ;
Let thy good Spirit ne'er depart,
Nor hide thy presence from my heart.   8

3. I cannot live without thy light,
Cast out and banish'd from thy sight :
Thine holy joys my God restore,
And guard me that I fall no more.   12

4. Tho' I have griev'd thy Spirit Lord,
Thy help and comfort still afford,
And let a wretch come near thy throne
To plead the merits of thy Son.   16

5. A broken heart my God, my King!
Is all the sacrifice I bring :
The God of grace will ne'er despise
A broken heart for sacrifice.   20

6. My soul lies humbled in the dust,
And owns thy dreadful sentence just :
Look down O Lord with pitying eye,
And save the soul condemn'd to die.   24

7. Then will I teach the world thy ways,
Sinners shall learn thy sov'reign grace,
I 'll lead them to my Saviour's blood,
And they shall praise a pard'ning God.   28

8. O may thy love inspire my tongue!
Salvation shall be all my song,
And all my pow'rs shall join to bless
The Lord, my strength and righteousness ‡.   32

‡ The 17th verse, concerning the sacrifice of a broken heart,
have here transposed to make an easier connexion.

PSALM LI. ver. 3,—13. The first part.
Common Metre.

Original and actual sin confessed and pardoned.

LORD I would spread my sore distress
And guilt before thine eyes;
Against thy laws against thy grace
How high my crimes arise !   4

2. Shouldst thou condemn my soul to hell
And crush my flesh to dust,
Heav'n would approve thy vengeance well,
And earth must own it just.   8

3. I from the stock of Adam came
Unholy and unclean;
All my original is shame,
And all my nature sin †.   12

4. Born in a world of guilt I drew
Contagion with my breath,
And as my days advanc'd I grew
A juster prey for death.   16

5. Cleanse me O Lord! and cheer my soul
With thy forgiving love;
O make my broken spirit whole
And bid my pains remove !   20

† Or it may be read *My nature prone to sin.*

6. Let not thy Spirit quite depart,
Nor drive me from thy face;
Create anew my vicious heart,
And fill it with thy grace;   24
   7. Then will I make thy mercy known
Before the fons of men,
Backfliders fhall addrefs thy throne
And turn to God again.   28

PSALM LI. ver. 14,—17. The fecond part.
Common Metre.

Repentance and faith in the blood of Chrift.

O God of mercy! hear my call,
My loads of guilt remove,
Break down this feparating wall
That bars me from thy love: 4
   2. Give me the prefence of thy grace,
Then my rejoicing tongue
Shall fpeak aloud thy righteoufnefs
And make thy praife my fong.   8
   3. No blood of goats nor heifer flain
For fin could e'er atone;
The death of Chrift fhall ftill remain
Sufficient and alone.   12
   4. A foul opprefs'd with fin's defert
My God will ne'er defpife;
A humble groan a broken heart
Is our beft facrifice.   16

PSALM LIII. VER. 4,—6.

Victory and deliverance from persecution.

Are all the foes of Sion fools
Who thus devour her faints?
Do they not know her Saviour rules
And pities her complaints?   4

 2. They shall be seiz'd with sad surprise,
For God's revenging arm
Scatters the bones of them that rise
To do his children harm.   8

 3. In vain the sons of Satan boast
Of armies in array;
When God has first despis'd their host
They fall an easy prey.   12

 4. O for a word from Sion's King
Her captives to restore!
Jacob with all his tribes shall sing,
And Judah weep no more †.   16

PSALM LV. ver. 1,—8, 16, 17, 18, 22.
Common Metre.

Support for the afflicted and tempted soul.

O God my refuge! hear my cries,
Behold my flowing tears,
For earth and hell my hurt devise
And triumph in my fears.   4

† The first part of this Psalm is the same with the xivth.

2. Their rage is levell'd at my life,
My soul with guilt they load,
And fill my thoughts with inward strife
To shake my hope in God.   8

3. With inward pain my heartstrings sound,
I groan with ev'ry breath,
Horror and fear beset me round
Amongst the shades of death.   12

4. O were I like a feather'd dove,
And innocence had wings,
I'd fly and make a long remove
From all these restless things.   16

5. Let me to some wild desert go
And find a peaceful home,
Where storms of malice never blow,
Temptations never come.   20

6. Vain hopes and vain inventions all
To 'scape the rage of hell!
The mighty God on whom I call
Can save me here as well.   24

PAUSE.

7. By morning light I'll seek his face,
At noon repeat my cry,
The night shall hear me ask his grace,
Nor will he long deny.   28

8. God shall preserve my soul from fear,
Or shield me when afraid;
Ten thousand angels must appear
If he command their aid.   32

9. I cast my burdens on the Lord,
The Lord sustains them all;
My courage rests upon his word
That saints shall never fall.   36

10. My highest hopes shall not be vain,
My lips shall spread his praise,
While cruel and deceitful men
Scarce live out half their days‡.   40

PSALM LV. ver, 15, 16, 17, 19, 22. Short Metre.

Dangerous prosperity, or, *Daily devotions encouraged.*

LET sinners take their course
And chuse the road to death,
But in the worship of my God
I 'll spend my daily breath.   4

2. My thoughts address his throne
When morning brings the light,
I seek his blessing ev'ry noon,
And pay my vows at night.   8

3. Thou wilt regard my cries
O my eternal God‡
While sinners perish in surprise
Beneath thine angry rod.   12

‡ I have left out some whole Psalms, and several parts of
others, that tend to fill the mind with overwhelming sorrows
or sharp resentment, neither of which are so well suited to the
spirit of the gospel, and therefore the particular complaints of
David against Achitophel here are entirely omitted.

4. Because they dwell at ease
And no sad changes feel,
They neither fear nor trust thy name,
Nor learn to do thy will.   16

5. But I with all my cares
Will lean upon the Lord,
I 'll cast my burden on his arm
And rest upon his word.   20

6. His arm shall well sustain
The children of his love;
The ground on which their safety stands
No earthly pow'r can move.   24

PSALM LVI.

*Deliverance from oppression and falsehood, or, God's care
of his people in answer to faith and prayer.*

O Thou whose justice reigns on high
And makes th' oppressor cease,
Behold how envious sinners try
To vex and break my peace.   4

2. The sons of violence and lies
Join to devour me Lord!
But as my hourly dangers rise
My refuge is thy word.   8

3. In God, most holy, just, and true!
I have repos'd my trust,
Nor will I fear what flesh can do,
The offspring of the dust.   12

4. They wrest my words to mischief still,
Charge me with unknown faults;
Mischief doth all their counsels fill,
And malice all their thoughts.   16

5. Shall they escape without thy frown?
Must their devices stand?
O! cast the haughty sinner down
And let him know thy hand.   20

PAUSE.

6. God counts the sorrows of his saints,
Their groans affect his ears,
Thou hast a book for my complaints,
A bottle for my tears.   24

7. When to thy throne I raise my cry
The wicked fear and flee,
So swift is pray'r to reach the sky,
So near is God to me.   28

8. In thee, most holy, just, and true!
I have repos'd my trust,
Nor will I fear what man can do,
The offspring of the dust.   32

9. Thy solemn vows are on me Lord,
Thou shalt receive my praise;
I 'll sing, " How faithful is thy word,
" How righteous all thy ways!"   36

10. Thou hast secur'd my soul from death,
O set thy pris'ner free!
That heart and hand and life and breath
May be employ'd for thee.   40

PSALM LVII.

Praife for protection, grace, and truth.

My God! in whom are all the fprings
Of boundlefs love and grace unknown,
Hide me beneath thy fpreading wings
Till the dark cloud is overblown.   4

2. Up to the heav'ns I fend my cry,
The Lord will my defires perform;
He fends his angel from the fky
And faves me from the threat'ning ftorm.   8

3. Be thou exalted O my God!
Above the heav'ns where angels dwell;
Thy pow'r on earth be known abroad,
And land to land thy wonders tell.   12

4. My heart is fix'd, my fong fhall raife
Immortal honours to thy name;
Awake my tongue to found his praife,
My tongue, the glory of my frame.   16

5. High o'er the earth thy mercy reigns,
And reaches to the utmoft fky;
His truth to endlefs years remains
When lower worlds diffolve and die.   20

6. Be thou exalted O my God!
Above the heav'ns where angels dwell;
Thy pow'r on earth be known abroad,
And land to land thy wonders tell.   24

PSALM LVIII. as the 113th Psalm.

Warning to magistrates.

JUDGES, who rule the world by laws,
Will ye despise the righteous cause
When th' injur'd poor before you stands?
Dare ye condemn the righteous poor,
And let rich sinners 'scape secure,
While gold and greatness bribe your hands?   **6**

2. Have ye forgot, or never knew,
That God will judge the judges too?
High in the heav'ns his justice reigns;
Yet you invade the rights of God,
And send your bold decrees abroad
To bind the conscience in your chains.   **12**

3. A poison'd arrow is your tongue,
The arrow sharp the poison strong,
And death attends where'er it wounds:
You hear no counsels, cries, or tears;
So the deaf adder stops her ears
Against the pow'r of charming sounds.   **18**

4. Break out their teeth eternal God!
Those teeth of lions dy'd in blood,
And crush the serpents in the dust:
As empty chaff when whirlwinds rise
Before the sweeping tempest flies,
So let their hopes and names be lost.   **24**

5. Th' Almighty thunders from the sky,
Their grandeur melts, their titles die,
As hills of snow dissolve and run,
Or snails that perish in their slime,
Or births that come before their time;
Vain births! that never see the sun.   30

6. Thus shall the vengeance of the Lord
Safety and joy to saints afford,
And all that hear shall join and say
" Sure there 's a God that rules on high,
" A God that hears his children cry,
" And will their suff'rings well repay."   36

PSALM LX. ver. I,—5. 10,—12.

On a day of humiliation for disappointments in war.

Lord! hast thou cast the nation off?
Must we for ever mourn?
Wilt thou indulge immortal wrath?
Shall mercy ne'er return?   4

2. The terrour of one frown of thine
Melts all our strength away;
Like men that totter drunk with wine
We tremble in dismay.   8

3. Great Britain shakes beneath thy stroke
And dreads thy threat'ning hand;
O heal the island thou hast broke,
Confirm the wav'ring land!   12

4. Lift up a banner in the field
For thofe that fear thy name;
Save thy beloved with thy fhield,
And put our foes to fhame.   16

5. Go with our armies to the fight
Like a confed'rate god;
In vain confed'rate pow'rs unite
Againft thy lifted rod.   20

6. Our troops fhall gain a wide renown
By thine affifting hand;
'Tis God that treads the mighty down
And makes the feeble ftand.   24

PSALM LXI. ver. 1,—6.

Safety in God.

WHEN overwhelm'd with grief
My heart within me dies,
Helplefs and far from all relief
To Heav'n I lift mine eyes.   4

2. O lead me to the rock
That 's high above my head,
And make the covert of thy wings
My fhelter and my fhade!   8

3. Within thy prefence Lord
For ever I 'll abide;
Thou art the tow'r of my defence,
The refuge where I hide.   12

4. Thou giveſt me the lot
Of thoſe that fear thy name;
If endleſs life be their reward
I ſhall poſſeſs the ſame.   16

PSALM LXII. ver. 5,—12.

No truſt in the creatures, or, *Faith in divine grace and power.*

MY ſpirit looks to God alone,
My rock and refuge is his throne;
In all my fears, in all my ſtraits,
My ſoul on his ſalvation waits.   4

2. Truſt him ye ſaints in all your ways,
Pour out your hearts before his face:
When helpers faii and foes invade
God is our allſufficient aid.   8

3. Falſe are the men of high degree,
The baſer ſort are vanity;
Laid in the balance both appear
Light as a puff of empty air.   12

4. Make not increaſing gold your truſt,
Nor ſet your hearts on glitt'ring duſt;
Why will you graſp the fleeting ſmoke,
And not believe what God has ſpoke?   16

5. Once has his awful voice declar'd,
Once and again my ears have heard,
" All pow'r is his eternal due;
" He muſt be fear'd and truſted too."   20

                       I

6. For sov'reign Pow'r reigns not alone,
Grace is a partner of the throne;
Thy grace and justice, mighty Lord!
Shall well divide our last reward.   24

PSALM LXIII. ver. 1, 2, 5, 3, 4. First part.
Common Metre.

The morning of a Lord's day.

EARLY my God! without delay,
I haste to seek thy face;
My thirsty spirit faints away
Without thy cheering grace.   4

2. So pilgrims on the scorching sand
Beneath a burning sky
Long for a cooling stream at hand,
And they must drink or die.   8

3. I 'ave seen thy glory and thy pow'r
Thro' all thy temple shine;
My God! repeat that heav'nly hour,
That vision so divine.   12

4. Not all the blessings of a feast
Can please my soul so well
As when thy richer grace I taste
And in thy presence dwell.   16

5. Not life itself with all her joys
Can my best passions move,
Or raise so high my cheerful voice
As thy forgiving love.   20

6. Thus till my laſt expiring day
I 'll bleſs my God and King,
Thus will I lift my hands to pray,
And tune my lips to ſing.   24

PSALM LXIII. ver.6,—10. Second part. Com. Metre.

Midnight thoughts recollected.

'Twas in the watches of the night
I thought upon thy pow'r,
I kept thy lovely face in ſight
Amidſt the darkeſt hour.   4

2. My fleſh lay reſting on my bed,
My ſoul aroſe on high,
" My God, my life, my hope!" I ſaid,
" Bring thy ſalvation nigh."   8

3. My ſpirit labours up thine hill,
And climbs the heav'nly road,
But thy right hand upholds me ſtill
While I purſue my God.   12

4. Thy mercy ſtretches o'er my head
The ſhadow of thy wings,
My heart rejoices in thine aid,
My tongue awakes and ſings.   16

5. But the deſtroyers of my peace
Shall fret and rage in vain,
The tempter ſhall for ever ceaſe,
And all my ſins be ſlain.   20

6. Thy fword fhall give my foes to death,
And fend them down to dwell
In the dark caverns of the earth,
Or to the deeps of hell.   24

PSALM LXIII. Long Metre.

Longing after God, or, The love of God better than life.

GREAT God! indulge my humble claim,
Thou art my hope, my joy, my reft;
The glories that compofe thy name
Stand all engag'd to make me bleft.   4

2. Thou great and good, thou juft and wife!
Thou art my Father and my God,
And I am thine by facred ties,
Thy fon, thy fervant, bought with blood.   .8

3. With heart and eyes, and lifted hands,
For thee I long, to thee I look,
As travellers in thirfty lands
Pant for the cooling water-brook.   12

4. With early feet I love t' appear
Among thy faints and feek thy face;
Oft' have I feen thy glory there,
And felt the pow'r of fov'reign grace.   16

5. Not fruits nor wines that tempt our tafte,
Nor all the joys our fenfes know,
Could make me fo divinely bleft,
Or raife my cheerful paffion fo.   20

S ij

6. My life itself without thy love
No taste of pleasure could afford,
'Twould but a tiresome burden prove
If I were banish'd from the Lord.   24

7. Amidst the wakeful hours of night,
When busy cares afflict my head,
One thought of thee gives new delight,
And adds refreshment to my bed.   28

8. I 'll lift my hands, I 'll raise my voice,
While I have breath to pray or praise;
This work shall make my heart rejoice,
And spend the remnant of my days.   32

PSALM. LXIII. Short Metre.

Seeking God.

My God! permit my tongue
This joy to call thee mine,
And let my early cries prevail
To taste thy love divine.   4

2. My thirsty fainting soul
Thy mercy doth implore;
Not travellers in desert lands
Can pant for water more.   8

3. Within thy churches Lord
I long to find my place,
Thy pow'r and glory to behold,
And feel thy quick'ning grace.   12

4. For life without thy love
No relish can afford:
No joy can be compar'd to this
To serve and please the Lord.   16

5. To thee I 'll lift my hands,
And praise thee while I live;
Not all the dainties of a feast
Such food or pleasure give.   20

6. In wakeful hours at night
I call my god to mind;
I think how wise thy counsels are,
And all thy dealings kind.   24

7. Since thou hast been my help
To thee my spirit flies,
And on thy watchful providence
My cheerful hope relies.   28

8. The shadow of thy wings
My soul in safety keeps:
I follow where my Father leads,
And he supports my steps †.   32

---

† After I had finished the common metre of this Psalm I ob-
served several pious turns of thought in Dr. Patrick's version,
which I have copied in this metre, tho' with some difficulty,
because of the shorter lines.

PSALM LXV. I,—5. First part. Long Metre.

Publick prayer and praise.

The praise of Sion waits for thee
My God! and praise becomes thy house;
There shall thy saints thy glory see,
And there perform their publick vows.   4

2. O Thou! whose mercy bends the skies
To save when humble sinners pray,
All lands to thee shall lift their eyes,
And islands of the northern sea.   8

3. Against my will my sins prevail,
But grace shall purge away their stain;
The blood of Christ will never fail
To wash my garments white again.   12

4. Bless'd is the man whom thou shalt chuse,
And give him kind access to thee,
Give him a place within thy house
To taste thy love divinely free.   16

PAUSE.

5. Let Babel fear when Sion prays;
Babel! prepare for long distress
When Sion's God himself arrays
In terrour and in righteousness.   20

6. With dreadful glory God fulfils
What his afflicted saints request,
And with Almighty wrath reveals
His love to give his churches rest.   24

7. Then shall the flocking nations run
To Sion's hill and own their Lord;
The rising and the letting sun
Shall see the Saviour's name ador'd. 28

PSALM LXV. ver. 5,——13. The second part.
Long Metre.

Divine Providence in air, earth, and sea, or, *The God of nature and grace.*

THE God of our salvation hears
The groans of Sion mix'd with tears,
Yet when he comes with kind designs
Thro' all the way his terrour shines. 4

2. On him the race of man depends
Far as the earth's remotest ends,
Where the Creator's name is known
By nature's feeble light alone. 8

3. Sailors that travel o'er the flood
Address their frighted souls to God
When tempests rage and billows roar
At dreadful distance from the shore : 12

4. He bids the noisy tempests cease;
He calms the raging crowd to peace
When a tumultuous nation raves
Wild as the winds and loud as waves. 16

5. Whole kingdoms shaken by the storm
He settles in a peaceful form;
Mountains establish'd by his hand
Firm on their old foundations stand.   20

6. Behold his ensigns sweep the sky,
New comets blaze and lightnings fly;
The Heathen lands with swift surprise
From the bright horrours turn their eyes.   24

7. At his command the morning ray
Smiles in the east and leads the day;
He guides the sun's declining wheels
Over the tops of western hills.   28

8. Seasons and times obey his voice;
The ev'ning and the morn rejoice
To see the earth made soft with show'rs,
Laden with fruit and dress'd in flow'rs.   32

9. 'Tis from his wat'ry stores on high
He gives the thirsty ground supply;
He walks upon the clouds, and thence
Doth his enriching drops dispense.   36

10. The desert grows a fruitful field,
Abundant food the vallies yield;
The vallies shout with cheerful voice,
And neighb'ring hills repeat their joys.   40

11. The pastures smile in green array,
There lambs and larger cattle play;
The larger cattle and the lamb
Each in his language speaks thy name.   .   44

12. Thy works pronounce thy pow'r divine;
O'er ev'ry field thy glories shine;
Thro' ev'ry month thy gifts appear:
Great God! thy goodness crowns the year.　48

PSALM. LXV. First part. Common Metre.

A prayer-hearing God, and the Gentiles call'd.

PRAISE waits in Sion, Lord! for thee,
There shall our vows be paid;
Thou hast an ear when sinners pray;
All flesh shall seek thine aid.　4

2. Lord our iniquities prevail,
But pard'ning grace is thine,
And thou wilt grant us pow'r and skill
To conquer ev'ry sin.　8

3. Bless'd are the men whom thou wilt chuse
To bring them near thy face;
Give them a dwelling in thine house
To feast upon thy grace.　12

4. In answ'ring what thy church requests,
Thy truth and terrour shine,
And works of dreadful righteousness
Fulfil thy kind design.　16

5. Thus shall the wond'ring nations see
The Lord is good and just,
And distant islands fly to thee
And make thy name their trust.　20

6. They dread thy glitt'ring tokens Lord!
When figns in heav'n appear,
But they fhall learn thy holy word
And love as well as fear.   24

PSALM LXV. Second part. Common Metre.

*The providence of God in air, earth, and fea, or, The
blefting of rain.*

'Tis by thy ftrength the mountains ftand,
God of eternal pow'r!
The fea grows calm at thy command,
And tempefts ceafe to roar.   4

  2. Thy morning light and ev'ning fhade
Succeffive comforts bring;
Thy plenteous fruits make harveft glad,
Thy flow'rs adorn the fpring.   8

  3. Seafons and times, and moons and hours,
Heav'n, earth, and air, are thine;
When clouds diftil in fruitful fhow'rs
The Author is divine.   12

  4. Thofe wand'ring cifterns in the fky
Borne by the winds around,
With wat'ry treafures well fupply
The furrows of the ground.   16

  5. The thirfty ridges drink their fill,
And ranks of corn appear;
Thy ways abound with bleffings ftill,
Thy goodnefs crowns the year.   20

PSALM. LXV. Third part. Common Metre.

The blessings of the spring, or, *God gives rain*.

A Psalm for the husbandman.

Goon is the Lord, the heav'nly King,
Who makes the earth his care,
Visits the pastures ev'ry spring,
And bids the grass appear.   4

  2. The clouds like rivers rais'd on high
Pour out at thy command
Their wat'ry blessings from the sky
To cheer the thirsty land.   8

  3. The soften'd ridges of the field
Permit the corn to spring,
The vallies rich provision yield,
And the poor lab'rers sing.   12

  4. The little hills on ev'ry side
Rejoice at falling show'rs,
The meadows dress'd in all their pride
Perfume the air with flow'rs.   16

  5. The barren clods refresh'd with rain
Promise a joyful crop,
The parched grounds look green again
And raise the reapers' hope.   20

6. The various months thy goodnefs crowns;
How bounteous are thy ways!
The bleating flocks fpread o'er the downs,
And fhepherds fhout thy praife.   24

From the APOLLO PRESS,
by the MARTINS,
Jan. 5. 1782.

END OF VOLUME FIRST.

TABLE

TO FIND OUT ANY PSALM BY THE FIRST LINE.

The numerals refer to the volume, and the figures to the page.

A
	V. P.
ALL ye that love the Lord rejoice,	ii. 240
Almighty Ruler of the skies,	i. 71
Amidst thy wrath remember love,	i. 152
Among th' assemblies of the great,	ii. 46
Among the princes, earthly gods,	ii. 56
And will the God of grace,	ii. 47
Are all the foes of Sion fools,	i. 195
Are sinners now so senseless grown,	i. 84
Arise my gracious God,	i. 92
Awake ye saints to praise your King,	ii. 197

B
Behold the lofty sky,	i. 100
Behold the love, the gen'rous love,	i. 143
Behold the morning sun,	i. 102
Behold the sure Foundation-stone,	ii. 144
Behold thy waiting servant, Lord!	ii. 159
Bless O my soul the living God,	ii. 101
Bless'd are the sons of peace,	ii. 192
Bless'd are the souls that hear and know,	ii. 61
Bless'd are the undefil'd in heart,	ii. 148

Volume I.   T

	V. P.
Bless'd is the man, for ever bless'd,	i. 132
Bless'd is the man whose bowels move,	i. 161
Bless'd is the man who shuns the place,	i. 51
Bless'd is the nation where the Lord,	i. 134

C

Children in years and knowledge young,	i. 133
Come children learn to fear the Lord,	i. 141
Come let our voices join to raise,	ii. 83
Come found his praise abroad,	ii. 82
Consider all my forrows Lord!	ii. 163

D

| David rejoic'd in God his strength, | i. 108 |
| Deep in our hearts let us record, | ii. 16 |

E

| Early my God! without delay, | i. 205 |
| Exalt the Lord our God, | ii. 93 |

F

Far as thy name is known,	i. 175
Father! I bless thy gentle hand,	ii. 167
Father! I sing thy wondrous grace,	ii. 15
Firm and unmov'd are they,	ii. 179
Firm was my health, my days were bright,	i. 127
Fools in their heart believe and say,	i. 83
For ever blessed be the Lord,	ii. 218
For ever shall my song record,	ii. 58
From age to age exalt his name,	ii. 117
From all that dwell below the skies,	ii. 142
From deep distress and troubled thoughts,	ii. 187

G   V. P.

Give thanks to God, he reigns above, ii. 116
Give thanks to God, invoke his name, ii. 111
Give thanks to God most high, ii. 200
Give thanks to God the sov'reign Lord, ii. 198
Give to our God immortal praise, ii. 203
Give to the Lord ye sons of fame, i. 125
God in his earthly temple lays, ii. 57
God is the refuge of his saints, i. 170
God! my supporter and my hope, ii. 26
God of eternal love, ii. 115
God of my childhood and my youth, ii. 21
God of my life look gently down, i. 156
God of my mercy and my praise, ii. 123
Good is the Lord, the heav'nly King, i. 215
Great God! attend while Sion sings, ii. 50
Great God! how oft' did Israel prove, ii. 42
Great God! indulge my humble claim, i. 207
Great God! the heav'ns' wellorder'd frame, i. 104
Great God! whose universal sway, ii. 23
Great is the Lord, exalted high, ii. 196
Great is the Lord! his works of might, ii. 129
Great is the Lord our God, i. 173
Great Shepherd of thine Israel, ii. 43

H

Had not the Lord, may Israel say, ii. 177
Happy is he that fears the Lord, ii. 132
Happy the city where their sons, ii. 219

T ij

	V. P.
Happy the man to whom his God,	i. 131
Happy the man whose cautious feet,	i. 53
Hear me O God! nor hide thy face,	ii. 97
Hear what the Lord in vision said,	ii. 61
Help Lord! for men of virtue fail,	i. 79
He reigns, the Lord the Saviour reigns,	ii. 86
He that hath made his refuge God,	ii. 71
High in the heav'ns eternal God!	i. 144
How awful is thy chast'ning rod,	ii. 37
How did my heart rejoice to hear,	ii. 173
How fast their guilt and sorrows rise,	i. 88
How long O Lord shall I complain,	i. 81
How long wilt thou conceal thy face,	i. 82
How pleasant, how divinely fair,	ii. 49
How pleasant 't is to see,	ii. 193
How pleas'd and bless'd was I,	ii. 174
How shall the young secure their hearts,	ii. 152

I

Jehovah reigns, he dwells in light,	ii. 76
Jesus our Lord! ascend thy throne,	ii. 127
Jesus shall reign where'er the sun,	ii. 23
If God succeed not all the cost,	ii. 182
If God to build the house deny,	ii. ib.
I lift my soul to God,	i. 119
I 'll bless the Lord from day to day,	i. 139
I 'll praise my Maker with my breath,	ii. 226
I 'll speak the honours of my King,	i. 167
I love the Lord, he heard my cries,	ii. 139

	V. P.
In all my vast concerns with thee,	ii. 211
In anger Lord rebuke me not,	i. 64
In God's own house pronounce his praise,	ii. 241
In Judah God of old was known,	ii. 34
Into thine hand O God of truth,	i. 128
Joy to the world, the Lord is come,	ii. 90
I set the Lord before my face,	i. 90
Is there ambition in my heart?	ii. 188
It is the Lord our Saviour's hand,	ii. 100
Judge me O Lord and prove my ways,	i. 122
Judges, who rule the world by laws,	i. 201
Just are thy ways and true thy word,	i. 97
I waited patient for the Lord,	i. 157
I will extol thee Lord on high,	i. 126

L

Let all the earth their voices raise,	ii. 85
Let all the Heathen writers join,	ii. 155
Let children hear the mighty deeds,	ii. 39
Let ev'ry creature join,	ii. 237
Let ev'ry tongue thy goodness speak,	ii. 223
Let God arise in all his might,	ii. 8
Let sinners take their course,	i. 197
Let Sion in her King rejoice,	i. 171
Let Sion and her sons rejoice,	ii. 99
Long as I live I 'll bless thy name,	ii. 221
Lord! hast thou cast the nation off?	i. 202
Lord! I am thine; but thou wilt prove,	i. 93

	V.	P.
Lord! I am vile, conceiv'd in fin,	i.	190
Lord! I can fuffer thy rebukes,	i.	66
Lord! I efteem thy judgments right,	ii.	155
Lord! if thine eyes furvey our faults,	ii.	68
Lord! if thou doft not foon appear,	i.	78
Lord! I have made thy word my choice,	ii.	156
Lord! in the morning thou fhalt hear,	i.	63
Lord! I will blefs thee all my days,	i.	137
Lord! I would fpread my fore diftrefs,	i.	193
Lord of the worlds above,	ii.	52
Lord! thou haft call'd thy grace to mind,	ii.	54
Lord! thou haft heard thy fervant cry,	ii.	143
Lord! thou haft fearch'd and feen me thro',	ii.	206
Lord! thou haft feen my foul fincere,	i.	96
Lord! thou wilt hear me when I pray,	i.	62
Lord! 't is a pleafant thing to ftand,	ii.	75
Lord! we have heard thy works of old,	i.	164
Lord! what a feeble piece,	ii.	70
Lord! what a thoughtlefs wretch was I,	ii.	27
Lord! what is man, poor feeble man!	ii.	219
Lord! what was man when made at firft,	i.	72
Lord! when I count thy mercies o'er,	ii.	213
Lord! when thou didft afcend on high,	ii.	10
Loud hallelujahs to the Lord,	ii.	235
Lo! what a glorious Corner-ftone,	ii.	147
Lo! what an entertaining fight,	ii.	191

M   V. P.

Maker and sov'reign Lord,	i. 54
Mercy and judgment are my song,	ii. 94
Mine eyes and my desire,	i. 121
My God! accept my early vows,	ii. 214
My God! consider my distress,	ii. 161
My God! how many are my fears!	i. 59
My God! in whom are all the springs,	i. 200
My God! my everlasting hope!	ii. 18
My God! my King! thy various praise,	ii. 223
My God! permit my tongue,	i. 208
My God! the steps of pious men,	i. 151
My God! what inward grief I feel,	ii. 209
My heart rejoices in thy name,	i. 129
My never-ceasing songs shall show,	ii. 59
My refuge is the God of love,	i. 77
My righteous Judge! my gracious God!	ii. 216
My Saviour and my King,	i. 166
My Saviour, my almighty Friend!	ii. 19
My Shepherd is the living Lord,	i. 114
My Shepherd will supply my need,	i. 115
My soul, how lovely is the place,	ii. 51
My soul lies cleaving to the dust,	ii. 165
My soul! repeat his praise,	ii. 105
My soul! thy great Creator praise,	ii. 107
My spirit looks to God alone,	i. 204
My spirit sinks within me Lord,	i. 163
My trust is in my heav'nly Friend,	i. 67

N

	V. P.
No fleep nor flumber to his eyes,	ii. 190
Not to our names, thou only juft and true,	ii. 138
Not to ourfelves who are but duft,	ii. 136
Now be my heart infpir'd to fing,	i. 168
Now from the roaring lion's rage,	i. 111
Now I 'm convinc'd the Lord is kind,	ii. 25
Now let our lips with holy fear,	ii. 13
Now let our mournful fongs record,	i. 112
Now may the God of pow'r and grace,	i. 106
Now plead my caufe almighty God,	i. 142
Now fhall my folemn vows be paid,	ii. 6

O

O all ye nations praife the Lord,	ii. 141
O bleffed fouls are they,	i. 130
O blefs the Lord, my foul!	ii. 104
O Britain! praife thy mighty God,	ii. 229
Of juftice and of grace I fing,	ii. 96
O for a fhout of facred joy,	i. 172
O God my refuge! hear my cries,	i. 195
O God of grace and righteoufnefs,	i. 61
O God of mercy! hear my call,	i. 194
O God to whom revenge belongs,	ii. 78
O happy man whofe foul is fill'd,	ii. 183
O happy nation where the Lord,	i. 136
O how I love thy holy law!	ii. 153
O Lord, how many are my foes,	i. 60
O Lord, our heav'nly King,	i. 68

V. P.

O Lord our Lord, how wondrous great,   i. 70
O that the Lord would guide my ways,   ii. 160
O that thy ſtatutes ev'ry hour,   ii. 164
O thou that hear'ſt when ſinners cry,   i. 191
O thou whoſe grace and juſtice reign,   ii. 176
O thou whoſe juſtice reigns on high,   i. 198
Our God our help in ages paſt,   ii. 66
Out of the deeps of long diſtreſs,   ii. 185
O what a ſtiff rebellious houſe,   ii. 40

P

Praiſe waits in Sion, Lord! for thee,   i. 213
Praiſe ye the Lord, exalt his name,   ii. 195
Praiſe ye the Lord, my heart ſhall join,   ii. 224
Praiſe ye the Lord; 't is good to raiſe,   ii. 227
Preſerve me Lord in time of need,   i. 87

R

Rejoice ye righteous in the Lord,   i. 133
Remember Lord our mortal ſtate,   ii. 63
Return, O God of love, return,   ii. 69

S

Salvation is for ever nigh,   ii. 55
Save me O God! the ſwelling floods,   ii. 11
Save me O Lord from ev'ry foe,   i. 89
See what a living Stone,   ii. 146
Show pity Lord, O Lord forgive!   i. 189
Shine mighty God! on Britain ſhine,   ii. 7
Sing all ye nations to the Lord,   ii. 5

	V. P.
Sing to the Lord aloud,	ii. 45
Sing to the Lord Jehovah's name,	ii. 80
Sing to the Lord with joyful voice,	ii. 93
Sing to the Lord ye diſtant lands,	ii. 84
Songs of immortal praiſe belong,	ii. 128
Soon as I heard my Father ſay,	i. 124
Sure there's a righteous God,	ii. 28
Sweet is the mem'ry of thy grace,	ii. 222
Sweet is the work, my God, my King,	ii. 74

T

Teach me the meaſure of my days,	i. 155
Th'Almighty reigns, exalted high,	ii. 83
That man is bleſt who ſtands in awe,	ii. 129
The earth for ever is the Lord's,	i. 117
Thee will I love O Lord! my ſtrength,	i. 94
The God Jehovah reigns,	ii. 91
The God of glory ſends his ſummons forth,	i. 185
The God of our ſalvation hears,	i. 211
The heav'ns declare thy glory Lord,	i. 103
The King of ſaints how fair his face,	i. 169
The king, O Lord! with ſongs of praiſe,	i. 107
The Lord appears my helper now,	ii. 142
The Lord, how wondrous are his ways!	ii. 102
The Lord Jehovah reigns,	ii. 77
The Lord is come, the heav'ns proclaim,	ii. 87
The Lord my Shepherd is,	i. 116
The Lord of glory is my light,	i. 123
The Lord of glory reigns, he reigns on high,	ii. 76

V. P.

The Lord the Judge before his throne, i. 179

The Lord the Judge his churches warns, i. 182

The Lord, the sov'reign King, ii. 106

The Lord the Sov'reign sends his summons forth, i. 183

The man is ever bleit, i. 52

The praise of Sion waits for thee, i. 210

The wonders Lord! thy love has wrought, i. 160

Think, mighty God! on feeble man, ii. 64

This is the day the Lord hath made, ii. 145

This spacious earth is all the Lord's, i. 118

Thou art my portion O my God! ii. 151

Thou God of love, thou ever blest, ii. 169

Thro' ev'ry age, eternal God! ii. 65

Thrice happy man who fears the Lord, ii. 131

Thus I resolv'd before the Lord, i. 154

Thus saith the Lord, " The spacious fields, i. 180

Thus saith the Lord, " Your work is vain, i. 158

Thus the eternal Father spake, ii. 124

Thus the great Lord of earth and sea, ii. 125

Thy mercies fill the earth O Lord! ii. 157

Thy name almighty Lord, ii. 142

Thy works of glory, mighty Lord! ii. 120

'Tis by thy strength the mountains stand, i. 214

To God I cry'd, with mournful voice, ii. 36

To God I made my sorrows known, ii. 215

To God the great, the ever bless'd, ii. 114

To heav'n I lift my waiting eyes, ii. 171

	V. P.
To our almighty Maker God,	ii. 90
To thee before the dawning light,	ii. 150
To thee moſt holy and moſt high!	ii. 33
To thine almighty arm we owe,	i. 99
'Twas for thy ſake eternal God!	ii. 17
'Twas from thy hand, my God! I came,	ii. 208
'Twas in the watches of the night,	i. 206

V

Vain man, on fooliſh pleaſures bent,	ii. 118
Unſhaken as the ſacred hill,	ii. 178
Up from my youth may Iſrael ſay,	ii. 184
Up to the hills I lift mine eyes,	ii. 170
Upward I lift mine eyes,	ii. 172

W

We bleſs the Lord, the juſt, the good,	ii. 10
We love the Lord, and we adore,	i. 98
What ſhall I render to my God,	ii. 140
When Chriſt to judgment ſhall deſcend,	i. 181
When God is nigh my faith is ſtrong,	i. 89
When God, provok'd with daring crimes,	ii. 122
When God reſtor'd our captive ſtate,	ii. 180
When God reveal'd his gracious name,	ib. ib.
When Iſrael freed from Pharaoh's hand,	ii. 135
When Iſrael's ſins the Lord reproves,	ii. 41
When I with pleaſing wonder ſtand,	ii. 212
When man grows bold in ſin,	i. 147
When overwhelm'd with grief,	i. 203

2

	V.	P.
When pain and anguish seize me Lord,	ii.	167
When the great Judge, supreme and just,	i.	74
Where shall the man be found,	i.	125
Where shall we go to seek and find,	ii.	188
While I keep silence and conceal,	i.	133
While men grow bold in wicked ways,	i.	145
Who shall ascend thy heav'nly place,	i.	86
Who shall inhabit in thy hill,	i.	85
Who will arise and plead my right,	ii.	79
Why did the Jews proclaim their rage ?	i.	57
Why did the nations join to slay,	i.	56
Why do the proud insult the poor,	i.	178
Why do the wealthy wicked boast,	i.	150
Why doth the Lord stand off so far,	i.	76
Why doth the man of riches grow,	i.	176
Why has my God my soul forsook,	i.	109
Why should I vex my soul and fret,	i.	148
Will God for ever cast us off,	ii.	30
With all my pow'rs of heart and tongue,	ii.	204
With earnest longings of the mind,	i.	162
With my whole heart I 'll raise my song,	i.	73
With my whole heart I 'ave sought thy face,	ii.	162
With rev'rence let the saints appear,	ii.	60
With songs and honours sounding loud,	ii.	230
Would you behold the works of God,	ii.	119

Y V. P.

Ye holy fouls in God rejoice, i. 135
Ye iflands of the northern fea, ii. 89
Ye nations round the earth rejoice, ii. 93
Ye fervants of th' almighty King, ii. 134
Ye fons of men, a feeble race, ii. 72
Ye fons of pride that hate the juft, i. 177
Ye that delight to ferve the Lord, ii. 133
Ye that obey th' immortal King, ii. 194
Ye tribes of Adam join, ii. 231
Yet (faith the Lord) if David's race, ii. 62

INDEX.

Note, In this Table I have not directed to the several
parts or metres of the Pfalm left it fhould breed too
great a confufion of figures. What is fought in any
Pfalm may eafily be found by turning a leaf or two
backward or forward to the diftinct parts or metres.

If you find not what word you feek in this Table feek
another of the fame fignification, or feek it under
fome of the more general words, fuch as *God, Chrift,
Church, Saints, Pfalm, Prayer, Praife, Affliction,
Grace, Deliverance, Death, &c.*

A

ADAM the firft and fecond, their dominion, 8.
Afflicted, pity to them, 41, 35. and tempted, fupport-
ed, 55, 145, 146. their prayer 102, 143. faints happy 73, 119, xivth part, 94.
Afflictions, hope in them, 42, 13, 77. fupport and profit 119, xivth part; inftruction by them 94, 119,
xviiith part; fanctified 94, 119, xviiith part; courage in them 119, xviith part; removed by prayer
34, 107; fubmiffion to them 123, 131, 39, from
men. See *Perfecution.* In mind and body 143. try-
ing our graces 66, 119, xviith part, without rejec-
tion 89. Of faints and finners different 94. gentle
103. moderated 125. very great 102, 143, 77.

U ij

Aged faints' reflection and hope 7.

Allfeeing God 139.

Angels, guardian, 34, 91. all fubject to Chrift 89, 97. praife the Lord 103. prefent in churches 138.

Appeal to God againft perfecutors 7. concerning our fincerity 139. humility 131.

Afcenfion of Chrift 24, 68, 47, 110.

Affiftance from God 144, 138.

Atheifm practical 14, 36, 12. punifhed 10.

Attributes of God 36, 111, 145, 157.

Authority from God 75, 82.

B

Backsliding foul in diftrefs and defertion 25. reftored 51. pardoned 78, 130.

Blefling of God on the bufinefs and comforts of life 127.

Bleflings of a family 128, 131. of a nation 144, 147. of the country 65, 147. of a perfon 1, 32, 112.

Blood of Chrift cleanfing from fin 51, 69.

Book of nature and fcripture 19, 119, ivth part.

Britain's profperity 67. delivered from flavery 75. happinefs 147.

Brotherly love 133. reproof 141.

Bufinefs of life bleffed 127.

C

Care of God over his faints 34.

Charity to the poor 37, 41, 112. and juftice 15, 112. mixed with imprecations 35.

Chaſtiſement. See *Afflictions.*

Children praiſing God 3. made bleſſings 127, 128. inſtructed 34, 78.

Chriſt the ſecond Adam his incarnation, his dominion 8. his allſufficiency 16. his aſcenſion 24, 68, 110. the church's foundation 118. his coming the ſigns of it 12. his condeſcenſion and glorification 8. covenant made with him 89. firſt and ſecond coming, or his incarnation, kingdom, and judgment, 96, 97, 98. the true David 89, 35. his death and reſurrection 22, 16, 69. the eternal Creator 102. exalted to the kingdom 2, 21, 8, 72, 110. our example 109. faith in his blood 51. God and man 89. his Godhead 102. our hope 4, 51. his incarnation and ſacrifice 40. the king, and the church his ſpouſe 45. his kingdom among the Gentiles 72, 87, 132. his love to enemies 109, 35. his majeſty 97, 99. his mediatorial kingdom 89, 110. his obedience and death 69. his perſonal glories and government 45. praiſed by children 8. prieſt and king 110. his reſurrection on the Lord's day 118. our ſtrength and righteouſneſs 71. his ſufferings and kingdom 2, 22, 69. his ſufferings for our ſalvation 69. his zeal and reproaches *ibid.*

Chriſtians' qualifications 15, 24. church made of Jews and Gentiles 87.

Church, its beauty, 45, 48, 122. the birth-place of ſaints 87. built on Jeſus Chriſt 118. delight and

safety in it 27. deſtruction of enemies proceeds from
thence 76. gathered and ſettled 132. of the Gentiles 45, 47. God fights for her 46, 10, 20. God's
preſence there 132, 84. God's ſpecial delight 87,
132. God's garden 92. going to it, 122. the houſe
and care of God 131. of the Jews and Gentiles 87.
its increaſe 67. prayer in diſtreſs 80. perſecuted.
See *Perſecution*. Reſtored by prayer 85, 102, 107.
its ſafety in national deſolations 46. is the ſafety and
honour of a nation 48. the ſpouſe of Chriſt 46. its
worſhip and order 48. wrath againſt enemies proceeds thence 76.

Colonies planted 107.

Comfort, holineſs, and pardon, 4, 32, 119, xith and
xiith parts, and ſupport in God 94, 16. from ancient providence 77, 143. of life bleſſed 127. and
pardon 130.

Company of ſaints 16, 109.

Complaint of abſence from publick worſhip 42. of
ſickneſs 6. deſertion 13. pride, atheiſm, oppreſ-
ſion, &c. 10, 12. of temptation 13. general 102. of
quarrelſome neighbours 120. of heavy afflictions in
mind and body 143.

Compaſſion of God 103, 145, 147.

Communion with ſaints 106, 133.

Confeſſion of our poverty 16. of ſin, repentance, and
pardon, 32, 51, 38, 130, 143.

Conſcience tender 119, xiiith part, its guilt relieved
38, 32, 51, 130.

Contention complained of 12c.

Converse with God 119, iid part, 63.

Conversion and joy 126. at the ascension of Christ 110. of Jews and Gentiles 87, 1c6, 96.

Correction. See *Affliction*.

Corruption of manners general 11, 12.

Counsel and support from God 16, 119.

Courage in death 16, 17, 71. in persecution 119. xviiith part.

Covenant made with Christ 89. of grace unchangeable 89, 1c6.

Creation and providence 135, 136, 33, 1c4, 147, 148.

Creatures, no trust in them, 62, 33, 146. vain, and God allsufficient 33. praising God 148.

D

DAILY devotion 55, 139.

Day of humiliation for disappointments in war 6c.

Death and resurrection of Christ 16, 69. of saints and sinners 17, 37, 49. and sufferings of Christ 22, 69. deliverance from it 31. and pride 49. and the resurrection 49, 71, 89. courage in it 16, 17, 23. the effects of sin 90.

Defence in God 3, 121. and salvation in God 18, 61.

Delaying sinners warned 95.

Delight and safety in the church 48, 27, 84. in the law of God 119, vth, viiith, and xviiith parts, in God 63, 42, 73, 84, 18.

Deliverance begun and perfected 85. from despair 18.

from deep diftrefs 34, 40. from death 31, 118. from
oppreffion and falfehood 56. from perfecution 53,
94. by prayer 34. 40, 85, 126. from fhipwreck 107.
from flander 31. furprifing 126. from temptations
3, 6, 13, 18. from a tumult 118.

Defertion and diftrefs of foul 25, 13, 38, 143.

Defire of knowledge 119, ixth part, of holinefs 119.
xith part, of comfort and deliverance 119, xiith
part, of quickening grace 119, xvith part.

Defolations, the church's fafety in them 46.

Defpair and hope in death 17, 49. deliverance from
it 18, 130.

Devotion daily 55, 134, 141. on a fickbed 39, 6. See
Morning, Evening, Lord's day.

Direction and pardon 25. and defence prayed for 5.
and hope 42. See *Knowledge.*

Difeafe. See *Sicknefs.*

Diftrefs of foul, or backfliding and defertion, 25. relieved 51, 130.

Dominion of man over creatures 8.

Doubts and fears fupprefled 3, 31, 143.

Drunkard and glutton 107.

Duty to God and man 15, 24.

Dwelling with God. See *Heaven, Church, &c.*

E.

EDUCATION, religious, 34, 78.

Egypt's plagues 105.

End of the righteous and wicked 1, 37.

Enemies overcome 18. prayed for 35, 109. deftroyed 12, 76, 48.

Envy and unbelief cured 37, 49.

Equity and wifdom of Providence 9.

Evening Pfalm 4, 139, 141.

Evidences of grace, or felf-examination, 26. of fincerity 18, 19, 139.

Evil times 12. neighbours 120. magiftrates 11, 58, 82.

Exaltation of Chrift to the kingdom 2, 21, 22, 69, 72, 110.

Examination, or, evidences of grace 26, 139.

Exhortations to peace and holinefs 34.

F

Faith and prayer of perfecuted faints 35. in the blood of Chrift 51, 32. in divine grace and power 62, 130.

Faithfulnefs of God 89, 105, 111, 145, 146. of man 15, 141.

Falfehood, blafphemy, &c. 12. and oppreffion, deliverance from them 12, 56.

Family government 101. love and worfhip 133. bleffings 128.

Fears and doubts fuppreffed 3, 34, 31. in the worfhip of God 89, 99. of God 119, xiiith part.

Flattery and deceit complained of 12, 36.

Forgivenefs. See Pardon.

Formal worfhip 50.

Frailty of man 89, 90, 144.

Fretfulnefs difcouraged 37.

Friendſhip, its bleſſings, 133.

Funeral Pſalm 89, 90.

G

GENTILES given to Chriſt 2, 22, 72. church 45, 65,
72, 87. owning the true God 96, 98, 47.

Glorification and condeſcenſion of Chriſt 8, 45.

Glory of God in our ſalvation 69. and grace promiſed
84, 97, 98.

Glutton 78. and drunkard 107.

God all in all 127. allſeeing 139. allſufficient 16, 33.
his being, attributes, and providence, 36, 65, 147.
his care of ſaints 7, 34. his creation and providence
33, 104, &c. our defence and ſalvation 3, 61, 33,
115. eternal, and ſovereign, and holy, 93. eternal,
and man mortal, 90, 102. faithfulneſs 105, 111, 89.
glorified, and ſinners ſaved, 69. goodneſs and mercy
145, 103. goodneſs and truth 145, 146. governing
power and goodneſs 66. great and good 144, 68,
145, 147. heartſearching 159. our only hope and
help 142. the Judge 9, 50, 97. kind to his people
145, 146. his majeſty 97. and condeſcenſion 113,
114. mercy and truth 36, 103, 136, 89, 145. made
man 6. of nature and grace 65. his perfections 111,
36, 145, 147. our portion, and Chriſt our hope, 4.
our portion here and hereafter 73. his power and
majeſty 68, 89, 93, 96. praiſed by children 8. our
preſerver 121, 138. preſent in his churches 84. our
refuge in national troubles 46. our Shepherd 23.

his sovereignty and goodness to man 8, 113, 114. our support and comfort 94. supreme Governor 82, 93, 75. his vengeance and compassion 68, 97. unchangeable 89, 111. his universal dominion 103. his wisdom in his works 111, 139. worthy of all praise 145, 146, 150.

Good works 15, 24, 112. profit men, not God, 16.

Goodness of God 8, 103, 111, 145, 146.

Gospel, its glory and success, 19, 45, 110. joyful sound 89, 98. worship and order 48.

Government of Christ 45. from God 75.

Grace, its evidences, or, self-examination, 26, 139. above riches 144. without merit 16, 32. of Christ 45, 72. and providence 33, 56, 135, 136, 147. preserving and restoring 238. truth and protection 57. tried by affliction 17, 66, 125. and glory 84, 97. pardoning 130.

Guilt of conscience relieved 38, 32, 51, 130.

H

Harry saint and cursed sinner 1.

Harvest 65, 126, 147.

Health, sickness, and recovery, 6, 30, 31. prayed for 6, 38, 39.

Heart known to God 139.

Hearing of prayer and salvation 4, 10, 66, 102.

Heaven of separate souls and resurrection 17. the saints dwelling-place 24.

Holiness, pardon, and comfort, 4. desired 119, xith part, professed 119, iiid part, 139.

Hope in darkness 13, 77, 143. of resurrection 16, 71.
    and despair in death 17, 49. and prayer 27. for vic-
    tory 20. and direction 42. in afflictions 42, 143.
Hosanna of the children 8. for the Lord's-day 118.
Household. See *Family*.
Humiliation-day 10. for disappointment 60.
Humility and submission 131, 139.
Hypocrites and hypocrisy 12, 50.

                            I

IDOLATRY reproved 16, 125, 135.
Jehovah 68, 83. reigns 93, 96, 97.
Jews. See *Israel*.
Images. See *Idolatry*.
Imprecations mixed with charity 35.
Incarnation 96, 97, 98. and sacrifice of Christ 40.
Infants 139. See *Children*.
Instruction from God 25. from scripture 119, ivth and
    viith parts, in piety 34.
Instructive afflictions 94.
Intemperance punished 78. and pardoned 107.
Joy of conversion 126. See *Delight*.
Israel saved from the Affyrians 76. saved from Egypt,
    and brought to Canaan, 125, 136, 77, 105, 107.
    rebellion and punishment 78. punished and par-
    doned 106, 107. travels in the wilderness 107, 114.
Judgment and mercy 9, 68. day 1, 50, 96, 97, 98,
    149. seat of God 9.
Justice of providence 9. and truth towards men 15.
Justification free 32, 150.

K

King is the care of heaven 21.

King William and King George 75.

Kingdom of Chrift. See *Chrift.*

Knowledge defired 19, 119, ixth part.

L

Law of God, delight in it, 119.

Liberality rewarded 41, 112.

Life and riches, their vanity, 49. fhort and feeble 89, 90, 144.

Longing after God 63, 42.

Lord's day Pfalm 92, 118. morning 5, 19, 63.

Love of God to the righteous, and hatred to the wicked, 1, 11. to our neighbour 15. of Chrift to finners 35. of God better than life 63. of God unchangeable 106, 89. to enemies 109, 35. brotherly 133. and worfhip in a family *ibid.*

Luxury punifhed 78. and pardoned 107.

M

Magistrates warned 58, 82. qualifications 101. raifed and depofed 75.

Majefty of God 6%. See *God.*

Man, his vanity as mortal, 39, 89, 90, 144. dominion over creatures 8. mortal, and Chrift eternal, 102. wonderful formation 139.

Mariners' Pfalm 107.

Marriage, myftical, 45.

Volume I.   X

Mafter of a family 101.

Meditation 1, 63, 119, vth and vith parts.

Melancholy reproved 42. and hope 77. removed 126.

Mercies common and fpecial 68, 103. fpiritual and
temporal 103. innumerable 136. everlafting 136.
recorded 107. and judgment 9. and truth of God
36, 103, 89, 136, 145, 146.

Merit difclaimed 16.

Meffiah. See *Chrift.*

Midnight thoughts 63, 139, 119, vth and vith parts.

Minifters ordained 132.

Miracles in the wildernefs 114.

Morning Pfalm 3, 141. of a Sabbath 5, 19, 63.

Mortality of man 39, 49, 90. and hope 89. and God's
eternity 98, 101.

N

NATION's honour and fafety is the church 48. profperity 67, 144. bleffed and punifhed 107.

National deliverance 67, 75, 76, 124, 126. defolations, the church's fafety and triumph in them, 46.

Nature and fcripture 19, 119, viith part, of man 139.

New England Pfalm 107.

November the 5th 115, 124.

O

OBEDIENCE fincere 32, 18, 139. better than facrifice 50.

Old age, death, 90. and refurrection 17, 89.

Omnipotence, omnifcience, omniprefence, &c. See
God.

P.

Pardon, holinefs, and comfort, 4. of backfliding 78.
and direction 25. and repentance prayed for 38.
and confeffion 32. of original and actual fin 51.
plentiful with God 130.

Patience under afflictions 39. under perfecutions 37,
44. in darknefs 77, 130, 131.

Peace and holinefs encouraged 34. with men defired 120.

Perfections of God 111, 145, 147, 36.

Perfecuted faints, their prayer and faith, 35, 44, 74,
80, 83.

Perfecution, victory over and deliverance from it, 7,
53, 94. courage in it 119, xviith part.

Perfecutors punifhed 7, 129, 149. their folly 14. complained of 35, 44, 74, 80, 83. deliverance from
them 94, 9, 10.

Perfeverance 138. in trials 119, xviith part.

Perfonal glories of Chrift 45.

Peftilence, prefervation in it, 91.

Piety, inftructions therein, 34. See Saint.

Pity to the afflicted 41. See Charity, God.

Pleading without repining 39, 123. the promifes 119,
xth part.

Poor, charity to them, 15, 37, 41, 112.

Portion of faints and finners 11, 17, 37.

Poverty confeffed 16.

X ij

Power and majesty of God 89, 68, 145. See *God*.

Practical atheism 14, 36.

Praise to God from children 8. for creation and providence 33, 104. to our Creator 100. from all creatures 148. for eminent deliverance 34, 118. general 86, 145, 150. for the gospel 98. for health restored 30, 116. for hearing prayer 66, 102. to Jesus
Christ 45. from all nations 117, and prayer, publick, 65. for protection, grace, and truth, 57. for
providence and grace 36. for rain 65, 147. from
the saints 149, 150. for temporal blessings 68, 147.
for temptations overcome 18. for victory in war
ibid.

Prayer heard 4, 34, 65, 66. in time of war 20. and
hope of victory 20. praise, publick, 65. and hope 27.
in the church's distress 80. heard and Sion restored
102. and faith of persecuted saints 35, 37, 56. and
praise for deliverance 34. for repentance and pardon, &c. 38. See *Complaint*.

Preserving grace 138.

Preservation in publick dangers 46, 91, 112. daily 121.

Pride and atheism and oppression punished 10, 12,
and death 49.

Priesthood of Christ 51, 110.

Princes vain 62, 146.

Profession of sincerity and repentance, &c. 119, iiid
part, 139. false 50.

Promises and threatenings 81. pleaded 119, xth part.

Profperity dangerous 55, 73.

Profperous finners curfed 37, 49, 73.

Protection,truth,and grace, 57. by day and night 121.

Providence, its wifdom and equity, 9. and creation 33, 135, 136. and grace 36, 147. and perfections of God 36, its myftery unfolded 73. recorded 77, 78, 107. in air, earth, and fea, 35, 65, 89, 104, 107, 147.

Prudence and zeal 39.

Pfalm for foldiers 18, 60. for old age 71. for hufbandmen 65. for a funeral 89, 90. for the Lord's day 92. before prayer 95. before fermon ibid. for magiftrates 101. for houfeholders 101. for mariners 107. for gluttons and drunkards 107. for New England 107. for the 5th of November 115, 124. for Great Britain 67, 147. See *Morning*, *Evening*, &c.

Publick praife for private mercies 116, 118. for deliverance 124. worfhip, abfence from it complained of 42. worfhip attended on 122. prayer and praife 65, 84.

Punifhment of finners 1, 11, 37. and falvation 78, 81, 106. See *Affliction*.

Purpofes holy 119, xvth part.

Q

QUALIFICATIONS of a Chriftian 15, 24.

Quarrelfome neighbours 120.

Quickening grace 119, xvith part.

R

RAIN from heaven 135, 65, 147.

Recovery from sickness 6, 3c, 116.

Rejoicing in God 18. See *Joy*, *Delight*.

Relative duties 15, 133.

Religion and justice 15. in words and deeds 37.

Religious education 34, 78.

Remembrance of former deliverances 77, 143.

Repentance, confession, and pardon, 32. and prayer for pardon and strength 38. and faith in the blood of Christ 51.

Reproach removed 31, 37.

Resignation 39, 123, 131.

Resolutions, holy, 119, xvth part.

Restoring grace 138, 23.

Resurrection and death of Christ 2, 16. of the saints 16, 17, 49, 71. and death 49, 71, 80.

Reverence in worship 89, 99.

Revolution by King William 75.

Riches, their vanity, 49. compared with grace 144.

Righteous. See *Saints*.

Righteousness from Christ 71. See *Salvation*, *Pardon*, *Christ*.

S

SABBATH. See *Lord's day*.

Sacrifice 40, 51, 69. incarnation of Christ 40.

Safety in publick dangers 91. and triumph of the church in national desolations 46. in God 61. and delight in the church 27.

Saints happy and sinners cursed 31, 11, 119, ist part,
safety in evil times 12, 46. the best company 16.
characterized 15, 24. and sinners' portion 1, 17.
dwell in heaven 15, 24. punished and saved 78, 106.
God's care of them 34. reward at last 50, 90, 92.
and sinners' end 37, 1, 11. patience and world's hatred 37. chastised and sinners destroyed 94. die, but
Christ lives, 102. punished and pardoned 106, 107.
conducted to heaven 106, 107. tried and preserved
66, 125. afflictions moderated 125. judging the
world 149.

Salvation of saints 10. and triumph 18. and defence in
God 61. by Christ 69, 85.

Sanctified afflictions 119. last part, 94.

Satan subdued 3, 6, 13.

Scripture compared with the book of nature 19, 119,
viith part, instruction from it 119, ivth part, delight in it 119, vth and xviiith parts, holiness and
comfort from it 119, vith part, perfections 119, viith
part, variety and excellency 119, viiith part, attended with the Spirit 119, ixth part.

Seasons of the year 65, 147.

Seaman's song 107.

Secret devotion 119, iid part, 34.

Seeking God 63, 27.

Self-examination, or evidences of grace, 26, 139.

Separate souls, heaven of, 17.

Shepherd of saints is God 23.

Shipwreck prevented 107.

Sickbed devotion 6, 38, 39, 116.

Sickness healed 6, 30, 116.

Signs of Christ's coming 12, 96, &c.

Sin of nature 14. original and actual confessed and pardoned 51. and chastisement of saints 78, 106. universal 14.

Sincerity 19, 26, 32, 139. proved and rewarded 18. professed 119, iiid part.

Sinner cursed, and saint happy, 1, 11. and saints' portion 1, 17, 37, 50. hatred, and saints' patience, 37. destroyed, and saints chastised, 94.

Sins of the tongue 12, 34, 50.

Slander, deliverance from it, 31, 120.

Song. See Psalm.

Sorrows. See Affliction, Sickness, &c.

Souls in a separate state 17, 146, 150.

Spirit given at Christ's ascension 68. his teaching desired 119, ixth part, 51.

Spiritual enemies overcome 3, 18, 144. blessings and punishment 81. mindedness 119, iid part. See Saint, Grace, &c.

Spouse of Christ the King is the church 45.

Spring of the year 65. and summer 65, 104. and winter 147.

Storm and thunder 29, 135, 148.

Strength, repentance, and pardon, prayed for 38. from Christ 71. of grace 138.

Submiffion 123, 131. to Chrift 2. to ficknefs 39.

Succefs of the gofpel 19, 110.

Sufferings and death of Chrift 22. and kingdom of
Chrift 2, 22, 69, 110.

Summer 65. and winter 147.

Support and counfel from God 16. for the afflicted
and tempted 55. and comfort in God 94, 119, xivth
part.

Surety and facrifice Chrift our, 40.

T

TEMPTATIONS overcome 3, 18. in ficknefs 6. efcape
from them 25. of the devil 13. fupport under them
3, 55, 94.

Tempter. See *Satan.*

Tender confcience 119, xiiith part.

Thanks, publick, for private mercies 116, 118. See
Praife.

Threatenings and promifes 81.

Thunder and ftorm 29, 135, 136, 148.

Times, evil, 11, 12.

Tongue governed 34, 39.

Trial of our graces by afflictions 66, 125. of our hearts
26, 139.

Triumph for falvation 18. and fafety of the church in
national defolations 46. at the laft day 149.

Troubles. See *Afflictions, Temptations.*

Truft in the creatures vain 62, 146.

I

Truth, grace, and protection, 57, 145, 146. See *God, Faithfulness.*

Tumult, deliverance from it, 118.

V

VANITY of man as mortal 39, 89, 144. of life and riches 40.

Vengeance and compassion 68. against the enemies of the church 76, 149.

Victory hoped and prayed for 20. over temptations 6, 18, 144. over temporal enemies 18. and deliverance from persecution 53.

Vineyard of God wasted 80.

Unbelief and envy cured 37. punished 95.

Unchangeable God 89, 111.

Vows paid in the church 116. of holiness 119, xvth part.

W

WAITING for pardon and direction 25. for answer to prayer 85, 143, 130.

War, prayer in time of it, 20. disappointments therein 60. victory 18. spiritual 18, 144.

Warnings of God to his people 81.

Watchfulness 19, 141. over the tongue 39.

Weather 65, 107, 135, 147, 148.

Wicked. See *Sinner, Saint.*

Wickedness of man 14, 36, 51.

Wind. See *Providence, Seasons, Storm.*

Winter and summer 147.

Wifdom and equity of providence 9. of God in his
works 111.

Word of God. See *Scripture*.

Works of creation and providence 104, 147, 148.
and grace 19, 33, 111, 135, 136. good works profit men not God 16.

World's hatred and faints' patience 37.

Worfhip and order of the gofpel 58. delight in it 84.
with reverence 89, 99. daily 55, 134, 141. in a family 133. publick 63, 84, 122, 132. abfence from
it 42, 63.

Wrath and mercy from the judgment-feat 9. See
more in *God*, *Punifoment*, *Sinner*, *Vengeance*.

Z

Zeal and prudence 39.

Zion, its citizens 15. See *Church*.

From the APOLLO PRESS,
by the MARTINS,
Jan. 5. 1782.

www.ingramcontent.com/pod-product-compliance
Lightning Source LLC
Chambersburg PA
CBHW030801020726
47499CB00006B/1715